BLOOD AND BONE

CHAINS OF COMMAND BOOK 2

ZEN DIPIETRO

COPYRIGHT

COPYRIGHT © 2018 BY ZEN DIPIETRO

This is a work of fiction. Names, characters, organizations, events, and incidents are either products of the author's imagination or used fictitiously. Any resemblance to actual events, business establishments, locales, or persons, living or dead, is coincidental.

All rights reserved. No part of this publication may be reproduced, stored in a retrieval system, or transmitted in any form or by any means (electronic, mechanical, photocopying, recording, or otherwise) without express written permission of the publisher. The only exception is brief quotations for the purpose of review.

Please purchase only authorized electronic editions. Distribution of this book via the Internet or via any other means without the permission of the publisher is illegal and punishable by law.

ISBN: 978-1-943931-25-5 (paperback)

Published in the United States of America by Parallel Worlds Press

1

"Welcome to Officer Training School. You've worked hard to get here, but you'll work even harder to stay." Admiral Davies made this announcement sound like a warning, but her expression softened the statement.

Fallon looked to Hawk on her left, then Raptor and Peregrine to her right.

Yeah, they were ready.

They'd worked hard at the academy. The classes had been difficult and the physical training had been grueling, but the four of them coming together with their very different backgrounds and personalities to become a team had been the biggest challenge.

Together, they would conquer OTS too.

At least the new recruits surrounding them weren't competition. Fallon and her team had already earned their spots in their future specialty schools. They'd also earned their spot as a Blackout team—the sub-unit of PAC intelligence that was so classified it didn't even officially appear on any records. Most people, if they'd even heard of it, assumed it was a myth.

They assumed wrong.

Training as black ops officers while training as the standard variety of officer would be Avian Unit's new struggle.

Fallon surreptitiously touched the bracelet she wore on her right wrist. The other three had identical bracelets. Peregrine had built proximity detectors into the thin pieces of jewelry, since such small devices were her specialty. Fallon wondered what would happen to them to make such a thing useful.

Even more, she wondered when it would happen.

PAC Command's covert intelligence office wasn't exactly brimming with information about their journey into Blackout. Admiral Krazinski told them what he wanted them to know when he wanted them to know it. Outside of that, all they could do was wait.

Meanwhile, she had to figure out how to be the leader of this group of very large personalities. Between that and all the regular things they were supposed to learn over the next eighteen months, she had her work cut out for her.

Admiral Davies went on, saying a lot of things about hard work, dedication, and serving the PAC. Fallon didn't need that particular pep talk, and judging from Hawk and Peregrine's restless shifting, they didn't either. Raptor was probably the most patient of them, standing still and attentive.

Raptor. She was still getting used to thinking of him by that name. Sometimes she still thought of him as Drew before she caught herself.

They still used the regular names they'd been assigned at the academy when they were in public, but otherwise, they used their code names.

She needed to think of him as Raptor, her teammate. Not Drew, the guy she still had intense feelings for.

He turned his head slightly to look at her. Maybe he'd noticed her attention on him, or maybe he just wanted to gauge her reaction to Admiral Davies' speech.

Fallon gave him a faint smile and focused her attention on the admiral.

They'd agreed to officially end their romantic relationship after the academy so that they could commit themselves completely to serving the PAC.

Unofficially...well, they'd slipped up once or twice. Maybe three times. Now that they were at OTS, though, they needed to focus entirely on their work. The people they were trying to become didn't have room in their lives for romantic commitments and divided loyalties.

Their lives would be complicated enough without all that.

Finally, the admiral began to wind down. "I'm sure you're all eager to settle into your new rooms and get acquainted with your roommates. As you may already know, residences are arranged based on communal living. Assignments were made according to specialty, to give you more in common—including your schedules. But I recommend you get to know as many of your fellow cadets as you can during your time here. Chances are, you'll cross paths with some of them in the future, and when you're moving from duty post to duty post, there's nothing like finding an old friend." The admiral paused and smiled. "And there's nothing like getting a duty assignment alongside an old enemy, either, so I recommend not making any of those."

The large, standing-room-only hall filled with light chuckles and a few teasing comments. For her part, Fallon looked to Hawk, giving him a pointed stare.

He returned a *who, me?* look, then snarled at her for good measure.

She smirked. He wasn't as disagreeable as he pretended to be. Mostly. He just didn't trust people and, therefore, preferred to keep them at arm's length by appearing angry and disagreeable.

Admiral Davies smiled. "We expect a lot from you, but don't forget that we're proud of this very talented group of people. Serving the PAC isn't always easy, and it always does my heart good to see so many young faces eager to do it nonetheless. Now, go get moved in. Your classes start in two days, and you'll definitely see me around campus. Some of you will even be in my classes. Dismissed!"

Fallon hated crowds. Deeply. Unremittingly. As people bumped into her from all directions as they shuffled toward the exits, she gritted her teeth. Clenching her fists, she steeled herself to remain patient and polite. When the crowd parted and space opened ahead of her, she rushed forward to put some space between her and the mass of people.

Hawk huffed out a breath as they broke loose. "Whew. Thought I was going to have to start throwing people."

Raptor laughed as they crossed the OTS campus. "I doubt that would have been a great way to start off your career as an officer."

"Probably not. I just hate crowds."

Raptor and Peregrine didn't seem bothered by it, but Fallon noted that she and Hawk had that particular dislike in common.

"At least I only have to share my living space with you three," Hawk said as they followed the path toward their dorm. "I don't think it would go well for any of these shiny-faced paragons of virtue if they had to share with me."

"I doubt there are many true paragons here," Raptor said.

Hawk seemed unconvinced. "Compared to me, they are."

He used his handprint to unlock the cabin, which had been pre-keyed. "Biggest room's mine! It's fair, since I'm the biggest one here."

Raptor grinned. "Entirely reasonable. Go pick yours out."

He clearly already knew that they were all exactly the same in size, number of windows, and amenities.

Rather than having large dormitories, OTS had cabins. Most of them housed eight or ten people, with the bedrooms arranged in a wheel pattern around a circular living and eating area. Some cabins were larger or smaller, probably depending on area of study.

Avian Unit had their own four-person cabin. Fallon had already dropped her belongings off that morning, and now she looked forward to doing a little unpacking and settling in before getting some sleep. It had been a long day.

Living together, she supposed, would get them used to each other faster than anything else would. She was curious about Peregrine and Hawk, who she'd only just started getting to know. She'd established a good relationship with Hawk, and had begun to forge a bond with

Peregrine, though she'd become very quiet and introspective recently. Withdrawn, even. Guessing that the transition into something unknown was making Peregrine tense, Fallon had quietly given her space to work things out for herself.

She went to pick up her bags while Peregrine poured a glass of water in the kitchen that adjoined the living room.

It was a nice enough space. Not luxurious, but far from institutional. Everything had a homey feel and was in good repair. A couch flanked by a pair of chairs ensured plenty of seating, and a holo-vid projector in front of it all would give them the opportunity for a little recreation every now and then. A voicecom terminal had been built into the wall where the living room transitioned into the kitchen. A functional space. No doubt it would serve them well for the next year and a half.

Hawk came back, looking disappointed. "All the rooms are the same. I started to think I was in a bad dream where the same thing repeats over and over."

"Oh, are they?" Raptor acted surprised. "Ah, well. I'm sure it will be fine."

To keep Hawk from seeing her smile, Fallon grabbed her stuff and hurried back to find an unclaimed room.

MOVING into her new room reminded Fallon of when she moved into her dorm at the academy. The items she brought were much the same, too. Throwing knives, bo staff, sword, some clothes, and personal grooming items. She'd brought her academy hooded sweatshirt with her, both out of fondness for her experience of the place and the fact that it was a darn good hoodie.

As she put her knife collection in the closet, she paused, then flipped open the box containing her blades. She took a long look at the newest addition—the prize for winning the knife-throwing competition at the end of her senior year. She had a lot of knives, but that one was particularly special because she'd earned it.

She closed the container then shut the closet door. She sat on the bed and surveyed her new digs. The room was larger than the one she'd had at the academy. The basics were the same—bed, closet, dresser, and a desk with a voicecom display. She had a good-sized window here, though, and the chair and the desk looked comfortable. She also had an adjoining necessary, which she'd share with whoever took the room on the other side. It would be nice not having to go down the hall for a shower.

Yep, this would do just fine.

Here she was, finally on the verge of becoming an officer.

She went back to her closet and opened it. She ran her hand down the gray sleeve of the PAC uniform hanging inside. The material had some stretch to it and breathed well. Plus, it came in two pieces rather being a bodysuit, so it would be comfortable.

She'd tried it out when no one had been around.

The sound of a door opening got her attention and someone came through the bathroom.

Raptor appeared. "Oh, hello. So you're my new neighbor."

Apparently, he'd chosen the room next to hers. She wasn't sure how to feel about that, so she decided to work at feeling nothing at all. If she worked at it hard enough, surely it would become second nature.

"Seems so," she agreed.

"At least we're used to each other's living habits." He paused, an odd look coming over his face. Apparently, he hadn't entirely reconciled his thoughts in a platonic direction, either.

Good. It wasn't just her.

They'd adjust. They just needed a little time.

A loud voice came from behind Raptor. "Hey, preppy boy, do you have an extra comb? I can't find...hey, where did you go?"

Hawk poked his head into Fallon's room. "Oh, there you are. Did you bring an extra comb?"

Raptor's uncertainty faded, and he returned to his usual, good-humored self. "Probably. Let's go look. If not, I'm sure the commissary will have that kind of thing."

They left her room, talking about combs, socks, and dermacare patches.

This living situation would take a little getting used to.

FOUR MODULES, each of which would last four months, made up the entirety of the OTS curriculum. At the end of the first week of module one, Fallon returned to the cabin to find it empty.

She didn't mind getting a little silence and solitude. After three years at the academy of living either alone or with Raptor, having four big personalities under one roof had proven to be a bigger adjustment than she'd expected.

The day after moving into the cabin, Fallon woke up to find her towels missing. A room-by-room check of the cabin resulted in her discovering them on Hawk's bedroom floor.

She found the perpetrator himself in the kitchen, preparing himself a feast that was fit, at least size-wise, for a giant.

"Why are my towels in your room?" she asked, trying to keep her tone from sounding too demanding.

Maybe he had a good reason for using her towels. All three of them. And then not putting them in the processor.

"Because I used them," he said.

"Right. But why?"

"Because I realized I meant to buy towels when I got here. Then I didn't. And I needed a shower, so I went looking."

"Okay. So why did you take all of them? I only have three."

"Because they're tiny. It takes a lot to dry all this." He put his hands on his hips and posed provocatively.

She fought back a sigh, trying to remain patient. "Yeah, thinking about that makes me wonder if I even want them back now. But why didn't you put them in the processor and return them? They're all damp, and probably smelly, on the floor of your room."

"Forgot. Sorry. Feel free to grab 'em yourself."

She stared at him. "After you just reminded me that you rubbed your junk on them? No way. Just return what you've borrowed, in the condition you found it. And next time, ask first."

"You want me chasing you around the cabin, naked and dripping?" He seemed to like that idea a little too much.

"No!"

"Well, then." He smiled smugly, as if he'd won an argument.

Frustrated, she shot him a glare. "Buy yourself some towels today, before your next shower. Return mine, clean and folded. And plan ahead before you get naked, so you can ask if you can borrow something."

He shrugged nonchalantly. Apparently he'd bored of her, and was determined to focus all his attention on his giant meal.

"Don't make me set booby traps in my room," she warned.

"You wouldn't." He looked up at her cautiously.

She crossed her arms and glowered.

Sighing, he said, "Fine. I'll clean your little towels and get some of my own. Satisfied?"

No. She wasn't. But she doubted she could convey to him that the borrowing wasn't a problem so much as the method of having done so.

She suspected such nuances would take time.

For now, she only said, "Fine. And make me a sandwich too, while you're at it."

On the first day of classes, Fallon dragged her feet getting back to the cabin. After the classes were done, Hawk had said something vague about having some stuff to do, and that he'd be back late. Peregrine had slipped away without a word, but Fallon hadn't gotten the feeling that she was going back to the cabin.

Raptor was, though, and Fallon didn't want to be alone with him.

Not that she didn't trust him. Or herself. They were perfectly capable of controlling themselves. They'd agreed that their arrival on campus marked a fresh start to their vow of having a platonic relationship.

She just felt like that would be a lot easier if they weren't alone together.

She decided to visit the commissary. Hawk had eaten most everything in the kitchen. Again. It was his turn to stock up on groceries, but she'd stop in and grab herself some shelf-stable items she could stash in her room.

Of course, he probably had some special sense that would alert him to the presence of food in her room, but she'd started giving some serious thought to her booby trap threat.

She filled a cart with packets and pouches, then added some fresh fruits and vegetables that didn't need to go into the cooler.

If she bought some chips and ate them that night, Hawk wouldn't even have a chance to get any of them.

Chips it was, then.

She turned down the aisle that had salty snacks, only to see Raptor look up at her with an expression of surprise.

"Oh, hi," he said. "I was just—"

"Trying not to starve with Hawk as a roommate?"

He laughed. His unease faded and suddenly they were just themselves again.

They could do this. No problem.

"What did you get?" He stepped closer and peered into her cart. "Ah, nice. I'll have to grab some tango fruit too. Those look good. Hey, if Hawk's going to be out, why don't we buy stuff to make a nice dinner? Maybe we could get Peregrine to help us prepare it, and it might pull her out of her shell a little."

"Yeah. What do you think that's about? I've been thinking it's just that the unfamiliar makes her uncomfortable."

He pursed his lips thoughtfully. "I was thinking homesickness. She didn't have time to go home to Zerellus before OTS started."

"True." Fallon had visited her family, and she assumed Raptor had visited someone. Hawk had disappeared for a while and said nothing at all about it, which was entirely normal for him. "That's a good thought."

He shrugged. "I have one of those every now and then."

"What should we make for dinner, then?"

"I saw some really fresh-looking fish. Should we go look?"

"Sure," she agreed.

They shopped, assembled the makings of a nice dinner, and returned to the cabin, and kept it all entirely platonic. He could have been Hawk or Peregrine, and she'd have treated him no differently.

Except for when they started walking to the cabin, she almost started to bump him playfully with her hip, out of habit.

Whoops. She caught herself at the last second.

Yeah, the platonic thing still needed a lot more work. Either she felt awkward and mistrustful of herself, or she got too comfortable and fell under his spell of humor, charm, and honesty.

Had the distance between them shrunk? Somehow they were right next to each other. Had he done that, or had she?

She subtly shifted to the right, putting more space between them.

"I hope Peregrine will be there," she said brightly, to cover the lapse.

"Me too," he agreed, just a little too forcefully.

"You're here." Fallon felt relief sweep through her when she saw Peregrine in the living room, sitting on the couch.

"I am." Peregrine said nothing more, but she studied the bags they carried.

She stood and helped put things away.

Fallon smiled, hoping Peregrine was settling in and ready to re-engage with the rest of the team.

But then Peregrine turned to leave when everything had been put away.

"Hang on," Fallon said. "We're going to make fish and roasted vegetables for dinner. Do you want to help?"

Peregrine shook her head. "No, thanks. I ate at the mess hall."

"Oh. Okay. If you change your mind…" Fallon closed her mouth. Peregrine had already disappeared down the hallway toward her room.

She sighed.

Raptor patted her on the shoulder. "We'll keep trying. But in the meantime, we're going to have a nice meal. Then we'll eat it. And we won't save any for Hawk."

She laughed and started to lean into him with her shoulder.

Scrap.

Living with him was turning out to be a minefield.

She put on her game face. It was just a meal. They could cook together without anything funny going on.

Determined, she reached for a cutting board.

It hadn't been the most auspicious start to their living together, but OTS had been a big change from life on the academy campus, so Fallon didn't intend to worry. Yet.

One week after the start of OTS classes, Fallon arrived back at the cabin to find herself alone. Should she make dinner for everyone? It seemed like the right choice, but she'd made two such efforts since the night she'd cooked with Raptor. Both times, Peregrine had disappeared into her room, and Hawk had loudly complained about the food being too spicy, even though he ate his portion and everything else that was left over.

Nah. They could fend for themselves or take their own turns at cooking. Or maybe they'd gone to eat at the cafeteria, which was often called the mess hall. Which didn't sound at all appetizing, though the food she'd tried there had been quite good.

Maybe the others were staying out to study for the next day's classes or getting to know some new classmates.

She dropped her backpack onto a chair and went to the kitchen for some water. As she drank it, she tried to decide how to spend the evening.

Recreation was out of the question. She simply had to decide what avenue of study would benefit her most the next day.

"Procedures class is tomorrow. I'll work on that." She liked the subject. Learning how PAC installations handled daily routines and emergency situations interested her.

She also liked the way her words fell into the empty room without Hawk to make some mildly insulting remark or Peregrine to wordlessly ignore her.

For a moment, she missed the academy and its easygoing students. The academy had been tough in its own way, with a great deal of competition and a wide breadth of subjects to study.

Here, the focus was much sharper, but so was the competition. On her first day of class, she'd found that rather than study information as it was presented, cadets studied ahead to learn the subject matter beforehand.

Apparently, impressing instructors and staying ahead of the others earned the choicest assignments and determined an officer's career trajectory.

That was fine. She wasn't actually in competition with the other cadets, since her trajectory had already been set, but she'd have no trouble keeping up. She was well on her way to memorizing all the texts for this module. With a little effort, she'd be done soon and would remain at the top of the class.

Even though her career was already mapped out, she still needed to continue to prove to Krazinksi that she deserved to be part of Blackout.

She washed her glass and set it on the drainboard. Picking up her backpack, she headed for her bedroom. Maybe later she'd get some dinner at the cafeteria. For now, she'd work on getting a jump on the next day's classes.

Halfway down the hall, she suddenly felt like she wasn't alone. She paused to listen, but no one had entered the cabin.

Eyeing the doorway to her room, she began walking again. She kept her steps even and unhurried as she silently set her backpack on the floor and tensed her body, preparing for a fight.

As soon as she stepped into the doorway, she saw him. A man, probably a few years older than her. Japanese or maybe Korean. That was a surprise.

She registered those facts even as she lifted her hands to defend herself.

"Stand down, cadet." He crossed his arms and leaned against the window in a casual posture.

Cautiously, she edged into the room. Nothing appeared to be missing or out of place. "Who are you?"

His lips quirked upward and he glanced down at the ground.

It was an unexpectedly modest expression, and she didn't know what to make of it.

"My name's Minho. What Whelkin was to you at the academy, I will be to you here at OTS."

Most of the tension left her body, leaving curiosity in its wake. "So you're going to take me to obscure locations and kick my ass on a regular basis?"

He grinned. "Ross told me I'd like you. I can see why. But no. At least, not on a regular basis. You and your team already have most of the combat skills you'll need. My role is more of a…guide."

"A guide," she repeated.

"A mentor, if you want to think of it that way. Someone to teach you how to do this job you've signed up for and how to lead your team."

"You're one of *them*." She didn't say the word "Blackout" aloud, but she felt like she'd thought it so hard, it was written in the air between them.

"I am."

She looked at him more closely. He was nice-looking and obviously fit, though a little too thin. He couldn't have been more than twenty-five. Why would such a young person have this role?

"So you're only here for me? Not for the rest of my team?"

He lifted his chin and looked down at her, amused. "I'll be around for them too. But mostly you, especially at the beginning."

"So you're an instructor here?"

He shook his head. "No. I don't appear on any official documents relating to this campus. Nor will I be here all the time. But I'll be here when you need me, unless there's a good reason for me not to be."

"Unless you and your team get called up for an assignment," she translated.

He shrugged, but didn't correct her.

"Okay." She crossed her arms and affected a posture like his. If he wanted to ambush her in her room like some kind of pervert, he'd have to lead the conversation.

"Actually…" she countered herself, thinking aloud. "This is the second time I've come back to my room to find some older, wiser, guru lying in wait. You guys should change up your playbook."

Minho grinned again, looking boyish and annoyingly likeable. "Whelkin pulled the old attack-you-from-the-shadows thing when you first met?"

"It was more like stuffing me in a sack and hauling me around over his shoulder, but close enough. Why? Did he do it to you?"

He nodded. "I guess he likes to stick to the classics."

For some reason, that made her smile.

He brightened. "Aha, you're not humorless after all. For a minute there, I was starting to worry you were going to be a real drag."

"Would that matter? Your duties would be the same either way."

"Here's the first thing I'm going to teach you. If your job is going to be the same no matter what, why not make it fun? The truth is, sometimes that little bit of fun is the only thing that keeps you sane."

He cocked a finger at her. "Think about it. I'll be in touch."

He moved past her to the hallway.

"That's it?" she demanded.

He paused and looked back at her. "I'm not meeting the others yet. I should go before they return."

"Should I not tell them about you?"

He locked eyes with her for a long moment before speaking. "I'd rather you didn't, yet, but they're your team. You decide how to handle them." He started to leave again.

Quickly, she said, "About that. I think the fact that all four of us were selected but I was chosen as the leader might be rubbing one of my partners the wrong way. I thought our training missions had gotten us on the road to being a real team, but she's shutting me out. At first, I thought she was adjusting, but she hasn't snapped out of it. I don't think homesickness could explain it, either. If she were that tied to home, she wouldn't be planning on going into intelligence. The only reason I can think of is that she resents my being made the leader."

He shrugged. "It's up to you to prove to your teammates that you're the right choice."

"How do I do that?"

"You have to earn their trust. How you'll be able to do that, I don't know, but I'll help you as you go along. Good night, Fallon."

"Good night, Minho." She watched him go rather than walking him to the door. Somehow, it felt like the right thing to do.

When she heard the door close behind him, she sat on her bed. "Earn their trust."

She thought she already had. Maybe not.

Hawk had to trust her, to some degree. He knew she'd thrown the combat competition at the academy and given up the championship to protect him. Plus, they'd developed some rapport while drinking together at his favorite pub.

Ironically, his taking her towels indicated to her that he felt comfortable with her, which implied trust. He hadn't taken any personal items belonging to Raptor or Peregrine. Just her.

Likewise, she knew Raptor trusted her. Implicitly. She was certain of it.

Peregrine was a different story. She'd opened up a little before they'd left the academy, but since then, she'd closed right back up. The woman wasn't easy to know, which made it all the harder for Fallon to know if she should give Peregrine some time and space or confront her head-on.

So far, she'd been waiting it out, but that might be the wrong choice. At least now, she might be able to get some advice from someone who, presumably, had once gone though the same process of building a team.

She hoped Minho would make her life easier rather than harder, but she had her doubts. Things would only get harder the further she went into Blackout.

2

A HAND at the back of the classroom went up. A thin Atalan man asked, "If an officer follows all protocols and something is still smuggled onto a PAC space station, what are the consequences to the officer?"

The instructor, Captain Avares, smiled ruefully. "That's what we call a situational gray area. The officer's superior, in conjunction with PAC command, will complete an investigation. If the officer did in fact follow protocol and didn't miss any clues, it's the policy itself that might face disciplinary action. And by that, I mean some sort of adjustment." The captain smiled again. "But if the officer only technically followed protocol or missed some indicator that should have been caught, the consequences depend on the findings. Anything from an informal reprimand right up to decommissioning could occur. Fortunately, that's rare. No one likes to see that happen."

Fallon listened to Captain Avares, but surreptitiously watched her teammates. They shared all the same classes for this first four-month module, and the togetherness gave her an opportunity to simply observe them.

Hawk tended to sit staring at either the ceiling or some far-off point. He was listening, though, even when it seemed like he wasn't. Asking him some subtle questions after class had proven that he wasn't just zoning out.

Peregrine looked like she was attending a memorial service. She sat, stiff and straight, wearing a grim expression. She never asked questions.

Raptor, or Drew, as the other cadets knew him, made friends everywhere he went. He seemed to always be surrounded by general goodwill. His friendly smile and good humor made him well-liked.

Fallon, for her part, had fallen into a middle ground between her teammates. She was neither as easygoing and likeable as Raptor nor as standoffish and disagreeable-looking as Peregrine and Hawk.

She imagined that this made her bland. Nondescript.

Rather than seeing that as a bad thing, she decided it was a positive trait. If she put in some effort to be sociable, as she had at the academy, she could pass for an average cadet. Or an outgoing one, like Raptor. Or she could go a different way and become someone unapproachable, like Hawk.

She could become whatever she wanted others to perceive her as. That seemed ideal, to her way of thinking.

Wasn't it?

Minho had told her that it was up to her to figure out her team and learn how to lead them. To that end, she invited them out to dinner and drinks the night after Minho's visit.

She thought of it as a team-building exercise.

In order to embark on this quest, she'd done her research. Reviews from the voicecom and anecdotal recommendations from other students had factored into her decision. She wanted to find something as similar to the Blue Nine as possible. Hawk had found it during the academy, and it had been the place where they'd really started getting to know one another.

They'd had some great evenings there, drinking, talking, and insulting each other.

In the end, she settled on Lone Wolf Lowell's as their new watering hole. She gave it fifty/fifty odds that Hawk would replace it with a place of his own choosing, but it was a good enough fit for now. Besides, the name seemed to suit Hawk perfectly.

She hoped, anyway. Thus far, Peregrine seemed to follow Hawk's lead unless she had a reason not to. Fallon guessed that if she could convince Hawk that Lone Wolf Lowell's was the place to be, Peregrine might just stick around long enough for Fallon to make some inroads with her.

Distance to the bar from the OTS campus had been another important characteristic when selecting a place. The four of them would be able to walk to Lone Wolf Lowell's. They wouldn't need to pay for a taxi or be too worried about getting home okay if someone had one too many.

As they walked there, Raptor kept up a lively conversation. He didn't seem at all perturbed by Hawk's grunts or Peregrine's monosyllabic answers. Fallon tried to fill in with some responses here and there to make things less awkward, but she didn't have Raptor's ease. His confidence and charm made it seem effortless.

She decided not to tell them about Minho. Not yet. That would focus her teammates' attention on him when they needed to focus on one another.

At least, she felt like that was what they needed.

She'd completed her memorization of all the textbooks for the first module. With that out of the way, she could focus on Avian Unit. She only wished leading them could be as clear-cut as memorizing some books.

As they entered the pub, Hawk cast his gaze around, wearing a critical expression. There wasn't a great deal to see. Run-of-the-mill tables and chairs, barstools up against a long, high counter, and a bar stocked with hundreds, if not thousands, of colorful bottles. The most distinctive thing about the place's décor was the colorful pieces of abstract art that hung on the walls here and there.

Fallon held her breath, waiting for his judgment. If he hated it, he might turn around and walk right out. Hawk was a man of strong opinions and low tolerance for things he didn't like.

He tilted his head thoughtfully, shrugged, and strutted to a table in the back.

He strutted a lot. Maybe it was his size. It would be hard for him to be nondescript. Or maybe he had such a distinctive walk because he'd decided to make the most of his imposing physicality.

Hawk scanned the people they passed while Peregrine paid more attention to the exits as she followed. Raptor smiled and nodded at people who looked up as the four of them passed. He even offered a few casual greetings, which were cheerfully returned. If Fallon didn't know better, she'd think he must already know those people.

Or maybe he did. He made friends easily.

"It might do." Hawk's voice sounded dismissive, but something about the way he perused his menuboard suggested to Fallon that he liked it.

"No pretzel knots," he muttered.

She looked at her own menuboard. "They have more food than I'd have expected, though. They must be hiding a decent kitchen back there."

She looked toward the bar and the door that led back into the kitchen, but couldn't see anything.

Raptor pointed at his menuboard. "They have cheese biscuits. Those might be as good as pretzel knots."

Hawk grunted in response, frowning at his menu.

They punched in their drink and food orders and waited.

"Hang on," Hawk said. "You said you're buying, right?"

Fallon shrugged. "Sure."

He picked up his menuboard and stabbed his finger at it a few more times. When he set it back down, he gave her a wicked smile.

Fallon laughed. "Fair enough. Anyone else?"

She looked at Raptor and Peregrine, but Raptor only shook his head and smiled. Peregrine turned her head slightly to the left, then slightly to the right in an almost imperceptible shake.

Ugh.

No. Fallon immediately chastised herself for feeling exasperated. *I can't get impatient with her. I just have to figure her out.*

Their drinks arrived. After a long swig, Raptor asked, "So what do you all think of the first module?"

Hawk shrugged. "Boring. Some of the protocols are ridiculously fussy. But it's easy, compared to the academy."

"It's fine," Peregrine said.

Fallon smiled at Raptor, grateful for his help with conversation. "I think I'm done already."

Raptor and Hawk burst out laughing.

"Done?" Hawk asked.

"I mean, in terms of the material. I've read all the books and done all the research."

"What's that like?" Hawk asked. "Being able to remember stuff after just looking at it once."

She shrugged. She hadn't meant to make the conversation about her, but if they wanted to know about her, she wouldn't shy away from questions. "Great, mostly. Except for when it's not. I remember stupid stuff too. Like the ingredient list of the toasted oatmeal cereal you like, or the fine print on road signs. All it takes is for something to seem familiar or remind me in some way, and I see it again in my head, even though cereal ingredients are not useful or interesting to me in any way."

"Huh." Hawk rubbed at his scruff. His beard tended to grow in fast, but for some reason, he didn't have a doctor give him a simple treatment to retard its growth. Either he liked shaving or he liked growing a beard. "Are there other ways it can be annoying?"

"It's hard not to hold a grudge. I can remember a nasty comment just like someone's saying it to me again. Every word, every inflection. Even the person's expression and exactly how I felt. It makes it harder to forgive and forget." She looked down at the table, frowning thoughtfully. She'd never really thought about her memory being inconvenient. It had simply always been the way it was.

"Sometimes it's hard to sleep," she said slowly. "My mind keeps replaying things, thinking about things, even when I want it to be quiet."

Hawk nodded slowly. "I guess it's a blessing and a curse, then."

"I guess. I don't know of any other way of being, so to me, that's just what life's like." Fallon shrugged.

Peregrine didn't say anything, but Fallon saw something in her eyes. A spark of recognition or understanding. Or something along those lines. Peregrine shifted her gaze and the flicker disappeared.

It had been there, though. Fallon tucked the reaction away to explore later.

A server appeared with a tray of food. "Berdak stew?"

Hawk raised his hand and the server set the bowl in front of him.

The server shifted his attention to the others. "Steak?"

Hawk raised his hand again.

The server set the plate in front of Hawk.

"And the grilled fish?" the server asked.

Hawk shook his head. "Look, buddy, I'm going to help you out. Just set everything in front of me, and if it isn't mine, I'll give it to the correct person."

"Uh…right. Okay." Rattled, the server quickly placed the rest of the dishes in front of Hawk, before hurrying away.

Raptor chuckled. "You certainly have a way with people."

Hawk cut into his steak. "I get shit done."

"Yes, so I remember." Raptor grinned. "Can you really eat all this food?"

Thus far, the rest of them had received a basket of cheese biscuits. Everything else had been for Hawk.

"Watch me," Hawk said, chewing. "You're about to see something very special."

A different server arrived, passed out the rest of their food, and left again.

Fallon bit into a cheese biscuit. Cheese, garlic, salt, and everything that was good in the universe melted in her mouth. "Scrap, that's good."

Raptor reached for one and tried it. "Mm. They're *really* good. Think you'll be satisfied with these instead of your pretzel knots, Olag?"

Hawk grimaced at the other name he'd been assigned. They used their public identity names when they weren't alone. There had been a few slips, but they were getting better at it. Raptor referred to Hawk as Olag perhaps more often than he really needed to. He occasionally even teased Peregrine with her other name, too.

"Watch it, preppy boy." Hawk bit into a biscuit. "They'll do."

Fallon decided to interpret that as high praise. "So what do you all think of OTS in general, so far?"

"So far, so good," Raptor said. "Frankly, it's easier than I thought. I mean, it's a lot of memorization, so it takes effort, but it's nothing like the intense academic classes at the academy."

"Too much bowing," Hawk mumbled, not looking up from his food.

Fallon and Raptor laughed.

"Did that somehow take you by surprise?" Raptor asked, amused.

"No. It's just annoying. A duck of the head for that person, a bow from the shoulders for that one, a deep bow from the waist for another. And it's all damn day long, like I'm doing some damn dance show to entertain everyone."

Fallon smiled. Sometimes people at the academy had bowed, but it had been a courtesy instead of a strict requirement. Here, it was definitely required. "At least we don't have to bow to other cadets whenever we arrive or leave somewhere. That'd get tedious fast."

"I guess," Hawk allowed. "But there are a lot of teachers, instructors, and commissioned paper pushers around here. I probably do some kind of bow a hundred times a day."

"I'm sure it'll be second nature in no time. You'll barely be aware you're even doing it," Fallon predicted.

"Think so?" Hawk asked.

"Sure." She stopped abruptly. She'd been thinking about how natural all the bowing had been to her, since she'd grown up as the daughter of two PAC officers. But she couldn't exactly say that. For their collective safety, and that of the PAC, they'd continued to keep their past lives hidden.

"Things like that always become automatic," she said instead.

"What about you, Poppy?" Raptor asked, looking at Peregrine with an innocent expression as if he weren't intentionally using the flowery name.

She shrugged.

When she didn't say anything, Raptor pressed, "That's it?"

Peregrine let out a tiny sigh. "It's fine. I'm just not as good at the memorizing stuff. I'm more of a visual learner, you know, learning by doing."

Raptor nodded with understanding. "Ah, yeah, makes sense. I have to work at it too, not like Miss Fancypants Memory over there." He sent Fallon a wicked look. "We could practice together, quizzing each other and whatnot."

Fallon tried not to appear too eager for Peregrine's response, but she really hoped Raptor could re-engage her into the team.

Having her hovering on the fringes this way wasn't going to work long term.

Peregrine shrugged again. "Maybe."

She turned her full attention on her food, pointedly ending the conversation. Raptor looked to Fallon and they exchanged microscopic shrugs of uncertainty. Did her "maybe" mean maybe or just that she wanted to quit talking about it?

Hawk, for his part, seemed oblivious to the exchange, busy as he was working through all the food he'd ordered.

Fallon knew better, though. He only pretended to be oblivious. She'd come to realize that he liked to make people underestimate him. It worked very well, too.

She should talk to him about Peregrine. The two of them had known each other longer than they'd known either Fallon or Raptor. Maybe Hawk would help her understand what was going on with Peregrine. She'd tried to wait out whatever had caused her to withdraw, but she clearly needed to use more proactive measures.

Peregrine's halfhearted response put a crimp in the conversation, and they fell silent as they dug into their food. That turned out to be fortunate, because everything was fantastic.

Fallon started to offer Raptor a bite of her sandwich, then caught herself. No, that wasn't normal behavior for platonic teammates.

Things like that kept happening.

Subtly, she stole a glance at him as he ate. Why did he have to look so perfect? All the lines of his face and the set of his shoulders and the way he sat were all just...so damn perfect.

She should talk to Minho about her dilemma. He'd surely have some wisdom to share.

But when would she see him again? It wasn't like he'd given her his details so she could call him on the voicecom whenever she needed something.

One thing at a time. She'd just have to keep working through.

Maybe that was the point of OTS, even more than the learning of procedures and policies and how to behave as an officer. Or maybe that would just be the point of it for her, personally.

Hawk signaled to a passing server. "Can I get another basket of biscuits here?"

The server nodded. "I'll have those right out for you."

Raptor laughed. "Seriously? After all this, you're going to add more biscuits? Can you even eat all that?"

Hawk nodded. "Oh, yeah. See, it helps to change up the flavor profiles. Then your taste buds don't get bored."

"Taste buds?" Raptor asked. "What about your stomach? I couldn't eat half of all that without feeling sick."

Hawk shrugged. "Lightweight."

Fallon and Raptor finished eating around the same time, then Peregrine finished. They sat and watched Hawk eat. And eat. And continue to eat. At some point, it started to feel more like performance art, but he did indeed eat every bit of his food, then nabbed a lone biscuit left from the basket the others had shared.

"We should get back," Hawk said. "I have a bunch of crap to memorize." He paused. "Just let me put in an order for some cheese biscuits to go, first."

Fallon was so impressed by the immensity of his eating that she didn't even mind paying the rather large bill for the food.

Plus, he looked so happy strutting back to the cabin with his bagful of biscuits.

It made her smile.

When they got back to the cabin, Fallon waited until Hawk went to his room, then quickly followed and softly knocked on his door.

"Yeah," his voice came through the door.

Since she didn't care for yelling through a door, she took that as an invitation to enter.

Hawk sat on the edge of his bed, peeling off his socks.

"Ahhh." He splayed his bare toes on the floor. "That's better. So what do you want?"

Rather than take his blunt question personally, she simply answered it. "Have you talked to Peregrine recently?"

He shrugged. "She's not talking much."

"Not even in private?"

"Not really. We've had a few brief conversations, but it was all matter-of-fact stuff about OTS. She's not exactly one to bare her soul."

Fallon walked around to the other side of his bed and sat, then stretched out, putting her head on the pillow.

"Uh, that's my bed," he pointed out.

"Yeah. It's just like mine. Comfy."

He sighed. "What's it going to take to get you out of here? I had plans to get fully naked, and that's going to happen in about five minutes, whether you're here or not."

"I only get five minutes?" She put her arms behind her head.

"Most everyone else would get about ten seconds."

"Most? What about the outliers?"

"I'd bounce their asses out of here as soon as they put a foot in my room."

"Ah, so I'm special, then."

He twisted around to look down at her. "We're down to four and a half minutes. Is this really how you want to spend your time?"

She grinned up at him. "Maybe. It's fun. And if you don't have anything more helpful to say about Peregrine, then I might as well needle you until it's time to cover my eyes and run."

He snorted. "Like you would. You'd be blinded by my hulking masculinity and have to hold yourself back from making sexual advances."

She giggled, and the giggles grew into an all-out belly laugh. "Hulking masculinity, huh? I'll have to remember that."

"Fine. If it will get you to leave faster, I'll say I don't know what Peregrine's deal is. Where I come from, you don't go poking people's sore spots. You mind your own damn business and let them deal with theirs."

She sat up, serious now. "But it's my job to watch out for you all."

"Tough cookies for you." He smirked. "I guess it's good I wasn't chosen as team leader."

"I'm sure they know what they're doing when they create a team. But if you ever have stuff going on, like Peregrine apparently does right now, you need to tell me about it. We have to trust each other, and you have to let me do my job. Okay?"

"So if I'm having deep feelings of inadequacy and fears of failure, I should say something?"

"Yes."

He grinned. "As if I'd have feelings of inadequacy. But consider it duly noted. I do, however, have a callus on my big toe that is driving me batshit—think you could handle that for me?"

He turned and stretched his leg out so that his big, surprisingly not-stinky foot was hovering over her face, like an ugly, fleshy angel.

"Gross. No!" She rolled off the bed and scrambled to her feet. "Keep that away from me."

"So you draw the line at foot care. Got it." He nodded once.

"If you were wounded or something, then maybe." She moved toward the door. "But you can handle your own pedicures."

"Glad we got that cleared up. Thanks for stopping by. Don't let the door hit you on the ass as you leave."

She shook her head and smiled. "Maybe I should hit you on the ass on my way out."

He grabbed the bottom of his shirt and paused before pulling it up over his head. "Now we're back to your unwanted sexual advances."

Laughing, she went back to her room. She hadn't made any inroads on figuring out Peregrine, but she enjoyed Hawk more and more the longer she knew him.

3

THE DAY after dinner at the pub, Fallon walked back to the cabin alone. Raptor wanted to meet up with a new friend; Hawk had claimed utter starvation and gone off in search of food, and Peregrine had slipped away without a word.

She hoped to find Peregrine at the cabin so she could confront her about her recent detachment. Fallon's initial instinct to let Peregrine sort it out herself didn't seem to be working. Fallon didn't want to let a significant issue fester, so it seemed like it was time to step in.

Hopefully, she could find a way to reach her teammate and reconnect the way they had after their first mission together.

What had changed since then?

She adjusted the strap of her backpack on her shoulder as she passed a service outbuilding. As she got to the other side of it, a figure lunged out at her, fast and aggressive.

Since her hand was still on her backpack and it would hinder her in fighting, she slung it off and threw it at him as hard as she could, moving into a defensive position.

He caught it and grinned at her. Recognizing Minho, she straightened.

"Good reflexes," he said.

"Thanks," she said dryly, and resumed course toward her cabin.

"Aw, you're not mad, are you?" he asked as he followed.

"No."

He held her backpack out to her.

"You carry it," she told him.

"Is this how you treat a superior officer?" he asked, a trace of humor in his voice.

"Not in general. But I feel like making an exception for you is the right decision." She fixed him with a pointed stare.

"They didn't tell me you were so cranky. I thought we were getting to be friends after you smiled last time."

"I saw you for maybe five minutes last time. I'm not cranky. I just don't know what your agenda is."

"I'm just doing my job," he said. "I don't have an agenda."

"Everyone has an agenda. Even if it's an altruistic one, it's an agenda nonetheless."

He grabbed her arm and she stopped short.

"You sure you want to do that?" she challenged.

He let his hand fall, but placed himself directly in her path. She watched his brown eyes appraising her. "Okay," he said. "Let's get to know each other."

She raised her eyebrows at him.

"I haven't earned your trust. I get it. Believe it or not, that's a good thing. Would you have challenged me back during your first year of the academy, or would you have bowed politely and done as you were told?"

She thought back to her younger self, arriving on the academy campus and hurrying to become the model student.

He saw the answer in her face and smiled. "I think that will be your first lesson from me."

Confused, she asked, "What is?"

Still smiling, he said, "It's not much of a lesson if I do all the work for you. Now, let's go back to your cabin and get to know each other."

His word choice amused her. "You sound like you're hitting on me."

He laughed, but his amusement quickly faded into seriousness. For a moment, he looked melancholy.

She wondered what he'd thought of to cause that. She took her backpack from him and started walking again. "All right. I'll make us some tea. I have a local Japanese blend I brought from home. You're Japanese, right?"

"Korean." He walked beside her, looking entirely casual. He didn't look like a Blackout agent. He looked like any other student or young officer. Like her, he appeared younger than whatever his age must actually be.

On the other hand, if he'd been easily identifiable as a Blackout officer, it would mean he was a really bad one.

"Japanese, Korean, close enough," she said.

"Don't let my grandmother hear you say that," he warned.

She laughed. "I meant that both are from the same planet, same continent, same geographic region. That kind of thing."

"I know. I'm kidding." He smiled, looking friendly.

"I can make coffee instead," she said.

"No, the tea sounded good."

Did he think she was a jerk for not being more friendly? So far, she'd found him in her room, and he'd jumped out at her. Those weren't exactly friendly overtures. Just to be sure, she said, "I'm not a jerk."

"That's exactly what a jerk would say."

He gave her a long, accusatory look, then laughed.

They said little else on the rest of the walk to her cabin. Inside, she set her backpack against the wall, then went to the kitchen to make tea.

On second thought, she went to check all the rooms to ensure no one else was there, then returned to the kitchen.

"You're learning," he said, taking a seat at the bar on the opposite side of the kitchen counter. He could have sat at the table, but he'd chosen to be closer, where he could face her directly.

"Is that the point?" She filled a kettle with water. "To make me paranoid?"

"I wouldn't call it paranoia. I'd call it vigilance. And no, that's not the point, though it's something you have to learn anyway. The further you go, the more you learn, the more you'll realize there's no such thing as safety."

"Okay." She leaned against the countertop while the water heated.

"Okay, what?" Minho looked uncertain.

"Okay, teach me your ways, oh wise one."

He sighed, but smiled as he did so. "There you go. I read that you have a sense of humor. I'd started to wonder if that was an error. Glad to see it isn't."

"My file says I'm funny?" She perked up at that, wondering what else her file might say.

"Yes. And academically gifted, a champion at knife throwing, and an increasingly skillful pilot."

She retrieved the kettle and poured water over tea leaves to let them steep. "So what's your specialty?"

When he hesitated, she pressed, "You wanted to get to know each other, right?"

He acknowledged her with a tiny nod. "Mechanics."

"That could mean a whole bunch of things. Care to be more specific?"

"Not really. I tend to be as vague as possible. But I'll say mechanical engineering."

"Oh, you're a fixer/maintenance type." She'd expected his specialty to be one that she or her teammates of Avian Unit had. But she supposed it made sense for other teams to have different combinations of skill sets.

Interesting.

"In a way, I guess."

"Do you have a team?" she asked.

He held up a hand. "Hang on. You asked a question, so it's only fair that I get to ask one before it's your turn again."

"All right." She scooped the tea leaves out of the cups, then set one in front of him.

He took his time deciding on what to ask. He blew lightly on his tea and tasted it, looking thoughtful. "Do you like dancing and photography?"

Of all the things he could have asked, she never would have guessed he'd ask that. "Like, both, at the same time?"

"If that's how you do it. That would be interesting."

"Well, I don't. I've never done much of either, actually."

"Ah." He gazed into his teacup. "Too bad."

"Why?"

"Because those are hobbies of mine. I thought maybe we had one of them in common."

"Sorry." She put her hands around her cup, leaning against the counter. "So dancing and photography, huh?"

"Well, the dancing is just recreational, for fun. Nothing professional. I like to think the photography's pretty good, though."

She tried to imagine him dancing or waiting for hours for the sun to be at just the right spot to capture just the right image. "You're not what I expected."

"I get that sometimes," he smiled.

Suddenly, she felt like he and Raptor would get along well. "From cadets?"

He shrugged. "In general."

"So, my turn. Same question. Do you have a team?"

"All Blackout officers are assigned to a team right from the start."

"So where's your team?"

He held up a finger. "That's a different question. I believe it's my turn to ask something."

"Fine."

"I'll let you ask one more thing today, but only if you answer this one, and then demonstrate the answer."

"Demonstrate?"

He fixed her with an unblinking stare. "Those are the terms."

Should she agree? What did he mean? What if he asked her about dancing or something again and wanted her to show him some moves?

Well...whatever. Even that would be worth it to get some insight from an actual Blackout officer.

"Deal. Ask."

"What's your favorite combat style?"

She was fond of her bo staff. And her sword. She also enjoyed the proper, pure forms of various martial arts. But when it came down to it, her favorite had always been fighting one on one, hand to hand, with nothing but her mind and body to rely on.

"Mixed style close combat." Once the words had left her mouth, she recalled what he'd said about demonstrating. She didn't regret her answer, though. Sparring with him would tell her as much about him as it would about her.

Actually, it might tell her more about him, since he'd already viewed her service record.

He set down his cup. "Perfect. Let's go."

SINCE BEGINNING THE ACADEMY, Fallon had become accustomed to squaring off against opponents who used a different fighting style. Whelkin had preferred a combination of pressure points and quick, heavy force to devastating effect. Raptor, on the other hand, had a style she could only characterize as shoulder and hip heavy. He put his full body into contact, and it was effective. Hawk had the strength and efficiency of a tank.

Minho, on the other hand, fought just like her. Quick. Calculating. Hard to touch.

Not since her days of competing for titles had she faced someone with such a similar style. Of course, back in those days, those events required a participant to conform to its rules. The fighting Fallon and Minho did had no rule but survival, yet their style was the same.

Fallon ducked out of his reach, and he ducked out of hers in turn. She watched for his weak spots, and he watched for hers.

She struck, deflected, retreated, advanced, and couldn't gain the upper hand. She even gave up a few hits, letting him strike her hard in the chest or upper arm, in the hopes of gaining an advantage for one strike that would give her the advantage.

It didn't happen.

Strike. Counterstrike. Dodge. Repel. Feint. Sucker punch. Nothing worked.

For either of them.

As sweat dripped down her forehead and burned her eyes, she forced herself on, continuing to look for a weak point. A moment of poor timing. Anything.

He used a double palm strike to her chest to knock her back, but that didn't throw her. Her hands were already up to deflect his follow-up punch.

She immediately responded with a knife-hand attack to his throat, which he repelled.

And on they went.

She'd never had a bout go this long. It felt like hours. She gasped for breath like the air was full of sand. Another droplet of sweat ran into her right eye, making her vision blur.

She used her awareness of his spatial location to throw another punch at his solar plexus. He knocked her fist away a second too late, but it didn't matter. Her strikes no longer had any force. Her arms felt like rubber.

Her legs betrayed her, making her stumble into him. Instead of capitalizing on her moment of weakness, he fell under her weight.

They collapsed to the ground together, gasping, sweating, blinded, and beyond exhausted.

The world around her darkened. She couldn't get enough air. She was too tired to even lift her head. She simply lay there, limp and spent.

Without knowing how much time had passed, she finally opened her eyes and focused them, and realized she'd fallen partially across Minho.

He was as still as death.

Oh, scrap. Had she killed him?

She flailed frantically to get her hand to the pulse at the base of his neck, but her arm was not obeying the orders she sent it. It went too far one way, then too far the other way. Finally, she managed to get her fingers against his jugular.

His pulse thrummed, even and sure, against her fingers.

She sighed and went limp again, glad that she wouldn't have to try to find the energy to get to her comport so she could summon help for him.

Her, on the other hand…she wasn't sure she'd ever gain the strength to walk again.

A minute—or maybe many minutes—later, she felt his hand slide up her back and to her neck, then press against her skin.

"I'm not dead," she croaked.

"Good. Me neither." His voice sounded no better than hers.

Still, even as she became aware of his ribs underneath her shoulder, and her right elbow against something soft, she couldn't get up.

Neither could he, apparently.

Breathing was the extent of her capabilities.

Gradually, her strength returned, and she was able to appreciate the cool air in the outbuilding he'd taken her to.

Except it hadn't been an outbuilding. What had looked like a dedicated server hub or a satellite station had, in fact, been his own cabin. Which included a private dojo.

She never would have realized.

Without knowing how much time had passed, she finally came to her senses enough to realize that she was sprawled across him in an awfully intimate way. Far more intimate than their relationship indicated. Discomfort bled into her exhaustion, making her dig down deep to find the energy to move.

With a groan, she rolled over her left shoulder, which pressed into his chest. That probably didn't feel good to him, but he didn't make a sound. With another half-turn, she managed to roll off onto the padded floor. The only part of her still touching him was from the knees down, which felt merely circumstantial rather than intimate.

About thirty seconds later, Minho said, "Finally."

It took her about the same amount of time to answer, "Shut up."

It was far from her best. On another day, at another time, she'd have delivered a blistering blow to his ego and entire sense of self worth. At the moment, though, "shut up" was all she had.

A full minute later, she felt him move his leg and weakly kick her calf.

"Jerk." She summoned her leg to deliver a mighty kick to his shin, but she only succeeded in giving him a gentle bump.

Dammit.

He made a sound that sounded like an asthmatic cough at first, but then deepened and grew louder. He was laughing. An exhausted, weak laugh, but a laugh nonetheless.

She giggled, then laughed along with him.

They laughed together, long and loud, though exhausted.

Probably longer than necessary, but all things considered, it felt great to laugh.

With great effort, he managed to turn himself over and lift up on his forearms to look at her. "You're not going to be easy, are you?"

She let her head loll to the left so she could look at him. "Probably not."

He smiled, and in spite of his exhaustion, she noticed for the first time how good-looking he was.

"Good," he said. "Maybe that will keep you alive."

If he could lift his body, then so could she. She summoned every ounce of endurance she had and moved her arms back so she could lift herself from her elbows. "What does that mean?"

He glanced away, then resolutely looked at her again, all traces of amusement gone. "Remember when you asked about my team?"

"Yeah."

"I'm the only one left. That's why I'm able to be here to teach you."

As soon as Fallon had enough strength, she hurried back to her cabin. The others would notice if she'd been gone too long, and she wanted some time to process her latest interaction with Minho before telling them about him.

He'd eventually gotten to his feet, as she had, but he'd been reluctant to say more about his teammates. He seemed to regret his admission about them. Maybe he hadn't meant to tell her that yet. Or at all.

Regardless, she was left to think about why the mentor assigned to her was a Blackout officer whose team had died.

At least, she assumed he meant that they'd died. She couldn't imagine he'd meant something else.

Was he there to help her become a leader, as he'd said during their first meeting? Or was his wisdom intended to keep her from losing her own team?

It bothered her. She claimed a headache when the others were eating together and took some food back to her room. She didn't want to look at them while she considered how she'd feel if they died.

Just thinking about it felt like a betrayal.

She ate only a few mouthfuls, then pushed her plate away. She had no appetite. She couldn't tell the others about Minho yet. Not until she knew more about how his team had died, and why he'd been assigned to her.

She didn't want them feeling the way she felt right then. She wanted to insulate them against that.

Later, when her comport alerted her to a message from Raptor, she put the comport down without reading what he'd said. She'd claim she was already asleep when it came through. She couldn't tell him everything yet, but she hated the idea of lying to him, even if it was only a lie by omission.

Worst of all, whenever she thought of losing her team, she saw Raptor in her mind's eye and had a hard time breathing.

She couldn't lose any of them, but she especially couldn't lose him.

4

FALLON DIDN'T WAKE up with the soreness that she'd had when training with Whelkin at the academy. She and Minho had been too evenly matched for that. Her discomforts were all internal and nonphysical.

She'd failed to connect with Peregrine due to Minho's sudden appearance. Today had to be the day.

After a run and a quick breakfast, she attended class purely because she was supposed to. Doing so afforded her no benefit at all, since she'd already memorized all the information that would be covered during this first module.

Attendance had become a habit, borne out of her desire to be seen as a top student. She felt compelled to go to class in spite of its uselessness.

Was that a fault, or a virtue? She felt less and less like it was a good thing.

In truth, she was a bit bored by OTS. She'd expected something more transformative. She seemed to be just passing time, waiting for something more definitive to happen.

Maybe that was a lesson she was supposed to be learning.

Patience. Perseverance. Becoming a cog in the PAC machine meant complying with a tremendous amount of infrastructure.

Fine. It wasn't like she had a choice. But it was damned boring. She sat listening to rehash and uninspired commentary. She tried to pretend to be engaged and listening, even when she felt like her brain cells were dying off out of sheer rebellion.

Finally, class ended. On the way out, Fallon put a hand on Peregrine's upper arm before she could disappear, as she tended to do these days.

When Peregrine turned her head, Fallon asked, "Can we talk?"

Peregrine showed no outward reaction. "Yes."

Fallon relaxed slightly, and only then did she realize she'd been tense about how Peregrine would react to a simple request.

Why? How had they drifted so far apart so quickly?

It just didn't make sense.

"Do you want to grab some lunch? Or we can just go back to the cabin." Fallon wanted Peregrine to be as comfortable as possible.

"I don't care." Peregrine stood, waiting for Fallon to decide.

She inwardly sighed, hiding her exasperation. "The cabin will be more private. Let's go there."

They began the trek across campus, and Fallon tried to channel Raptor and his easy way of talking to people. "How's class going? Would studying together help?"

Peregrine shrugged. "I'll work it out."

Fallon should wait. She should lead into the conversation artfully. But maybe this was the crux of it—Peregrine's refusal to rely on the others.

Instead, she plunged right in, then and there. "Why? Why do it on your own? I'm here to help. So are the others."

Peregrine kept looking forward, not sparing Fallon a glance. "That's how I've always done it."

"On your own? You never had anyone you could depend on?"

Peregrine opened her mouth like she was going to say something, then closed it again and shrugged.

"No, don't just shrug at me," Fallon said. "Tell me something. It's a yes or no question. Tell me yes or no. Stop shutting me out."

Peregrine's head lowered slightly. "I had one person. Ever. And he's very far away now."

Fallon took time to think about that before she responded to it. As terse as the response was, it gave real information.

Peregrine hadn't had many people to depend on in her life. Just one. A father or uncle, maybe. Perhaps a brother. That she hadn't had more people to rely on indicated that she'd faced hard times in her youth. That would be no surprise, given her hard exterior.

"Okay," Fallon said. "I get it. You're used to getting by on your own. Maybe asking for help is hard. Or maybe it feels pointless because you've asked for help in the past and no one answered. Or—I don't know—maybe it's just a pride thing. But you're shutting us out, and that's just not going to work. We were all really gelling as a team around the end of the academy. What happened between then and now?"

Peregrine started to shrug, but relaxed her shoulders. Her mouth turned down. "I don't like it here."

Fear sprang up in Fallon. If Peregrine washed out, where would that leave the rest of them? If she decided to quit and go back home, it would break the team. Whelkin had implied that if they weren't a team, they wouldn't be Blackout officers.

Carefully, Fallon said, "I don't love it either, to be honest. Probably for different reasons than you, but this isn't what I expected."

"Yeah," Peregrine agreed. "It's not what I expected."

"So what did you expect?"

"Something...more." Peregrine struggled for words. "I thought we'd keep building on the end of academy. Upping the action. This, what we're doing instead, feels like nothing. Protocol. Procedure. Memorizing. Nothing's happening."

"So...you're bored?" Fallon ventured.

Peregrine made a sound of frustration. "Not exactly. I mean, it's all I can do to memorize all this stuff. Import and export standards and sanctions for various solar systems. Trade doctrine. Treaty regulations. It's a lot of boring minutiae."

She stopped talking, but Fallon let the silence stretch, encouraging her to say more. They walked along in silence, except for their feet quietly moving along the pathway.

Peregrine continued, "I expected, you know, training missions and stuff. I could have buried myself in pointless minutiae on my home planet."

Peregrine looked around quickly to make sure there was no one to overhear, but nothing she'd said really revealed anything. Any other cadet might say the same thing.

Besides, there was no one else in their vicinity, either on the pathway, or walking across the grass between the paths.

"Okay," Fallon said. "I hear you. I expected training missions too. But here's what I think about this first module—I think it's boring as shit on purpose."

Peregrine perked up and looked at her.

Was that progress?

Fallon continued, "Being an officer is usually more mundane than exciting, right? Ensuring standards are met. Following protocol. We're all just cogs in the machine, right?"

She was saying, "right" too much. She was trying too hard. Taking a breath, she slowed down and made her voice more conversational. "So maybe this first module was designed to weed out the guts and glory types. To get rid of the people who can't handle boredom. I mean, imagine being stuck on some four-person outpost in the middle of dead space. Those rotations can last six months to a year. Officers have to be able to handle boredom, right?"

Scrap. She's said it again.

Peregrine didn't seem to notice. "Yeah. I guess."

"So if that's true, all we have to do is persevere. Mark time. Let it go by. You've waited out unpleasant things before, I'm sure. What was it like when you applied to the academy?"

Peregrine responded quickly. "What was it like for you?"

Fallon decided to withhold nothing. Peregrine needed to see pure honesty from her. "I was pretty sure I'd get in. I had the grades and the skills. I had the test scores. But even so, I was terrified. I'd put everything I had into getting to the academy. I had no fallback. There was nothing else for me. And waiting, holding my breath to see if I'd get recruited for..." she paused, since they were still in public. "For the thing I really wanted...every hour I had to wait was a boulder hanging around my neck."

Peregrine tilted her head to look at her. "Even with all the right things to put on your application, you were that worried? I'd have thought someone like you would never worry about a thing."

"Someone like me?" Fallon raised her eyebrows, entirely taken aback by that choice of words.

"Let's face it," Peregrine said flatly, "you and I are nothing alike."

"Aren't we?" Fallon challenged.

When Peregrine looked at her, she pressed onward. "We're after the same thing. We're willing to make the same sacrifices and take the same risks. Aren't we the same, regardless of our topical characteristics? And isn't that the point, that we all have our own strengths to bolster one another? To make us stronger as a whole?"

Peregrine blinked. Her features didn't exactly shift, but Fallon perceived surprise behind that carefully-sculpted disregard.

Maybe Peregrine had never thought of it that way.

Fallon pressed on. "You only had one person before. You have three now. Plus whoever you have back home."

They approached the door to their cabin. Before using her palm to open the door, she faced Peregrine. "When I fought Hawk for the championship, I realized something. He's mine. Mine to protect. Mine to get protection from. I will *never* hurt him. The same is true for you. You're mine to protect, Peregrine of Avian Unit. And you're mine to hide behind, too. We're more than family. More than married people. More than anything."

They stood face-to-face, eyes wide open. Fallon watched Peregrine and felt something shift. She couldn't describe it in words, but it was something important. Something that put them into a new alignment.

It was the beginning of something. She was sure of it.

"What about Raptor?" Peregrine asked.

"The same goes for him."

"Exactly the same? Are you still sleeping with him?"

Fallon felt her cheeks heat. How to assure Peregrine that she wouldn't give Raptor special treatment in a way that didn't violate his privacy? "I wouldn't..." she stopped. "I'm not..." she stopped again.

Was it her imagination or was Peregrine smiling? It was hard to tell.

Peregrine flipped her long, blond ponytail over her shoulder. "Relax. I couldn't care less who you sleep with. I was kidding."

Still blushing, Fallon asked, "You can kid?"

And there it was. A true smile. Sure, it was tiny. Imperceptible to most, maybe. But Fallon had no doubt.

"Of course I can. Do you think Zerellians aren't real humans or something?"

Fallon laughed and opened the door, stepping into the cabin. "I didn't know you were Zerellian."

"Really?" Peregrine closed the door behind her.

"I suspected. But I didn't know for sure."

"Aha. Well," Peregrine said. "Now you know."

"So I do." Fallon felt pretty good about it too. "And since we're sharing, I'm from Earth."

"Kinda figured." Peregrine smirked, dropping her backpack to the floor.

"Oh, now who's being racist?" Fallon grinned, knowing her Japanese features clearly marked her as an Earther, at least by blood.

Peregrine wasn't embarrassed. She seemed only amused.

There was a lot Fallon could learn from her. And a lot she could teach her, too. Fallon felt like a door had opened for her to do both.

Peregrine bent to look into the cooler, then sighed. "This is a disaster. Hawk eats everything. I swear, I'm going to buy my own cooler with a lock on it."

"I bet he'd still manage to get in there, even if he had to chew his way in," Fallon said. She'd eaten a lot of her meals in the mess lately because of Hawk's tendency to devour everything in sight. "The big oaf even stole my towels right after we got here. Left them all over his floor, too. The man has a lot to learn about living with others."

A strange sound came from Peregrine. If it were anyone else, Fallon would think it was a chuckle.

She squinted at Peregrine, who closed the cooler door with a look of disgust.

Peregrine said, "Have you ever had hendaya?"

"You mean the spicy noodles?"

"Yeah, but the real kind. Black bean noodles, not the starchy kind."

Fallon paused to think. "Actually, I don't think so."

"Let's go shopping. I'm in the mood for the real thing. And, I'll warn you, once you've had the real thing, you'll never go back to the Earthified kind."

Fallon tried to remember if she'd ever heard Peregrine voluntarily say so many words at once. "Teach me your Zerellian ways."

Again, she received that tiny smirk that indicated humor.

It felt like victory.

As they left the cabin together, Fallon reflected on her accomplishments during the short life of Avian Unit.

Her mission to Luna with Raptor had been exciting. Their first joint team endeavor had been challenging and thrilling.

But somehow…breaking through Peregrine's barriers felt like the greatest accomplishment Fallon had so far achieved as the leader of this team.

Fallon woke the next day re-energized. The previous day, she'd followed her instincts and forged a new bond with Peregrine. She'd have to work to keep building on that, but it was an auspicious new beginning. They'd eaten noodles, and while they hadn't exchanged more personal details, they had bonded over a general dislike for Hawk's seek-and-destroy habits when it came to food.

They'd also decided to resurrect the "hairy man-beast" nickname for him whenever he engaged in such behaviors.

With a spring in her step, she dressed, noted the details of her day as she'd organized them on the calendar, and gone forth to attend her boring classes with renewed vigor.

Only to find Admiral Krazinski standing in her path halfway across the campus.

It felt like kind of a special moment, in a terrible way, to have the person in charge of clandestine ops and making people disappear waiting for her.

How had he known she'd be alone?

She'd be thinking about that one for weeks. Years. She was sure of it.

But there she was, with a backpack on her shoulders, wearing a cadet's camo pants and white shirt, staring at the gray-haired, good-looking man who knew a trove of things that could get people killed.

"Hello, Emiko." He smiled, and in that smile, she saw a genuine humor over her name. They both knew it wasn't her real one. Nor was the codename he was refraining from using in public.

She bowed low, as befitted a mere cadet paying respect to an admiral of the highest order.

He might as well be a god. In relation to him, she was a flea. That was how far apart they were. There was no bow deep enough for the disparity of ranks between them.

Yet here they were.

"Hello, sir." She kept her voice calm and even, in spite of the jelly she felt in her stomach.

"Let's talk," he said.

She forgot all about attending classes that day.

ANOTHER OUTBUILDING, another clandestine meeting.

This was probably her life now.

Fallon sat across from Admiral Krazinski, even as she memorized the entire contents of the room from her peripheral vision.

"How's OTS, cadet?" he asked. For an old guy, he was good-looking and had a certain smoothness that few people did. It lent him an innate likeability.

She didn't fall for it.

"That depends, sir," she said.

"On what?"

"Whether you want an official account or my actual impressions."

He smiled. "Actual impressions, always, Fallon."

"It's boring as shit, sir." Where she got the guts to say something like that, she didn't know. Maybe it was that she suspected he'd see right through any attempt to be less than forthcoming.

Krazinski laughed. "Good."

"Is it, sir?"

He waved a hand. "Forget the bowing and the 'sir' stuff when we're in private. But yes, it's a good thing. And why do you think I'd say that?"

She answered immediately with the theory she'd suggested to Peregrine. "Because it's supposed to be, to weed out people who aren't prepared to deal with the boring stuff."

He nodded, smiling. "Precisely."

Since he was so pleased with her, she felt emboldened to press her luck. "Why send Minho to me?"

"Why do you think?" he asked again.

She was beginning to dislike his answers, which sounded more like some sort of psychotherapy, but she responded nonetheless. "I don't know."

"Then he hasn't done his job yet."

When she fell silent, he prompted, "Do you have more questions?"

"No."

"No?" He seemed surprised.

"You're only going to tell me what you're here to tell me anyway. So let's just get it all out, rather than pretend this is a real conversation."

Once the words were out, she held her breath. What had made her say something so bold? Just because he'd told her not to use honorifics didn't mean she could be so blunt.

But Krazinski laughed. "That's why you and I are going to get along so well. You can see through the bullshit."

She had nothing to say that wouldn't come out rude, so given her recent etiquette oversteps, she kept her mouth shut.

"How do you feel about some special training?" he asked.

"Great," she said immediately. "Let's do it."

He continued to smile. "Not just yet. You'll have two weeks between your first and second modules. We'll do it then."

"The whole team?" she ventured.

"Of course."

"Great," she repeated. When he didn't say more, she added, "You didn't come all the way here to ask me that. You could have had Minho tell me about it."

He made a self-deprecating gesture. "You're right. It's an excuse. Mostly, I just wanted to get my eyes on you. No, that's not it, precisely. I wanted to see how you're carrying yourself these days." He let out a slow breath and his smile faded. "I'm going to be brutally honest here, Fallon. My operatives are important to me as people. I care about them. I grieve when I lose them. But be that as it may, each operative represents a tremendous amount of time and effort expended to make them into an agent of Blackout."

He paused, but she said nothing, so he continued, "I've been at this for a long time. I've gotten good at picking out which ones aren't going to make it for the long haul. I wanted to get a good look at you to see if you're one of those."

"And?"

"And you don't need me to tell you that you're not one of those."

She nodded. "And my team? You'll be meeting with all the others, I assume?"

"Of course."

She lifted her chin. She didn't mind him evaluating her, but the idea of him being critical of her team made her defensive. "They'll be no different than me. I guarantee it."

"Do you?" He fixed her with a hard look.

She thought of Hawk. Of Raptor. Or Peregrine. "Absolutely."

He nodded. "Good. Dismissed."

Dismissed? Already? She had questions. She considered

ignoring the dismissal and asking them, but no. She'd pushed her luck enough already.

She stood, bowed, and left without a word.

Outside, she checked the chronometer on her comport. She couldn't show up at her class now. Entering this late would only draw attention to herself, while her lack of attendance was likely to go unnoticed by anyone but her team.

What should she do with her extra time?

It only took her a few seconds to decide.

She'd turn the tables on Minho. Chances were, he was around here somewhere. It would be interesting to see how he reacted to her showing up unannounced.

Laughing to herself, she ran back to her cabin.

5

Fallon hadn't started out the day with the intention of outspying a spy, but somehow, it had turned out that way.

She wasn't sorry. Actually, this was far better than listening to an instructor drone on about the finer points of docking and undocking protocols in deep space during an emergency.

Electricity crackled through her veins. She wished she could call in Hawk, Raptor, and Peregrine, because she wanted to get back that feeling of when they'd worked together. But they were in class, as they should be, and she hadn't yet told them about Minho.

She paused after entering the cabin and dropping her backpack on her bed. How should she go about catching him? What should she take with her?

Her thoughts went to the outbuildings on the campus. Minho had revealed one to her and Admiral Krazinski had revealed another. There could be others that served a secret purpose, too.

She'd start with the first one—the one Minho had taken her to. If she didn't find him there, she could stake out other buildings.

How strong would the security on that place be? She opened

her backpack and removed her infoboard. In its place, she put a digital lockpick kit.

It was a new hobby. She wasn't amazing at it yet, but she was learning.

Getting caught with the kit would probably get her into some serious trouble. On the other hand, wasn't it exactly the kind of thing she was supposed to be learning? She considered it to be self-study.

She tried to imagine what Krazinski would think.

She didn't think he'd disapprove.

Right, then.

She hurried out and headed for the faux outbuilding in question. When she arrived, it looked just as unassuming as it had before.

Just because she'd feel stupid if there were an easy solution right in front of her, she tried the door. Nope. Locked.

Since finding an open entry would be simpler than popping the security, she circled around, looking for access panels or vents, a back door, or a window.

Nothing.

Okay, she'd have to do it the hard way. It would be her first real-world test of her breaking-and-entering skill.

Judging by the fact that Minho and Whelkin had first introduced themselves to her using that method, she had a feeling it would be important in her intended line of work.

A closer look at the security lockout showed it to be a standard crytpocode lock. Basic. And why not? It wasn't like there was anything of interest in a maintenance outbuilding. No one would bother breaking into one, so putting a more complicated lock on it would only look out of place and suspicious.

She opened her backpack and fished the breakout device from her lockpick kit. Like most of the things in there, Hawk had helped her get it. He'd helped her start learning how to get past doors, too.

If she was lucky, she'd be able to isolate a range of likely codes and let the breakout device work through those.

She started with Standard numbers, then Standard letters, and when that didn't work, she started using alphabets from the other languages she knew.

No luck.

She'd have to go with a force-pulse. It was riskier in terms of detection, because Minho might have the system rigged to alert him of that kind of attack. And when he read the system log, he'd see it.

Since she didn't intend to hide the break-in, it would have to do.

After quickly looking around to make sure no one was around, she fitted the force-pulse to the security mechanism. As the force-pulse inductively drained energy from the lock, she admired Minho's choice of hideaway. The entrance faced away from the paths anyone was likely to take, reducing the risk of being seen.

That wasn't a lucky happenstance. Surely, whoever had set this place up had intentionally done that.

She wondered what all this place was used for. Maybe the inside would give her some clues. She hadn't seen much of it when Minho had brought her here for the purpose of sparring.

The force-pulse blinked its readiness, and Fallon pressed the activation button. She held her breath, then heard a faint click.

Cautiously, she tried the latch. When the door opened, she started to whoop, then muffled herself.

She returned everything to the backpack, then entered, quietly closing the door behind her.

Inside, she paused to listen. Minho could be there at that very moment. She heard nothing, though.

She stepped through the little dojo they'd used for their battle, then slipped down a narrow hallway. She paused again, listening, but heard nothing.

The hallway opened into an economy-sized kitchenette, which opened into a small living space.

So he lived here, whenever he was on campus. Interesting.

Very interesting.

Fallon paused to open the cooler and the cabinet door. Minho seemed fond of seafood and crunchy snacks.

She doubted that was useful information, but she tucked it away nonetheless.

The living space showed little evidence that anyone had been using it. A basic couch flanked a pair of basic chairs, all arranged around a plain, low table. He'd left out no menuboards, but the table had a voicecom display.

Should she look at it?

Had he looked at hers when he'd been in her room?

Undecided, she continued through to the bedroom. She froze.

Minho lay sprawled across a narrow bed, his eyes closed.

Sleeping. Surely he was sleeping. She had no reason to think he was dead.

Still...he was a Blackout officer, so, who knew? She edged closer to watch his chest. It rose and fell.

Okay, yeah, definitely sleeping. Whew.

She straightened quickly, realizing that she was hovering over this guy, who apparently preferred to sleep shirtless.

A mental image flared in her mind, depicting him waking up to find her leaning over his bare chest, staring at it.

He'd probably think she was a pervert.

Maybe she wouldn't feel so uncomfortable if he didn't have such a nice physique, or if he were less good-looking.

Nah. She'd feel weird about if it he were out of shape and homely too. It would just be a slightly different variety of weird.

That wasn't going to make her leave, though.

Now that she thought about it...yeah. This seemed about right as payback for ambushing her in her own bedroom.

She stepped back and put a hand on the chair that was

scooted up against the tiny desk. She turned the chair to face the bed and sat.

And waited.

Fallon didn't have to wait long. After just a couple minutes, Minho shifted and scratched his chin. Then his head turned toward her, and he slowly opened his eyes.

If he was surprised to see her, he didn't show it. He didn't move. He simply lay there, watching her.

She crossed her arms and stared right back at him.

"I give up," he finally said. "What are we doing?"

"Turnabout."

He kicked off the blanket that was tangled around his shins and sat up. The suggestiveness of the situation struck her, but she refused to acknowledge it. So what if she was in a man's bedroom while he sat on the bed half-naked? Apparently, this is what Blackout officers did, so she was going to do it.

She'd pretend this was totally normal, no matter how much effort it took.

"All right," he said agreeably. "Consider things turned. Now what?"

Since turning the tables and finding out more about him had been the entirety of her plan, she had to think fast.

"Tell me about your team," she said.

"Nope."

"Why not?"

He ran a hand through his hair. "First, because it's so classified that there's no official record that it even happened. Second, because it's personal. Third, because you aren't ready to hear it yet."

Those were good reasons, actually.

"Fine." She stood and turned to leave.

"Fine?" he echoed.

She looked at him over her shoulder. "Yep."

"Hang on," he said. He stood and pulled a shirt over his head, then gestured for her to go ahead of him to the living room.

When they got there, he gestured again, this time for her to sit, but she remained standing.

He shrugged. "Okay. We'll stand. I feel like you're here for a reason. You didn't come to ask about my team."

When she didn't answer, he pressed, "I'm actually here to help you. If you don't talk to me, that limits what I can do for you."

She hesitated. "Krazinski came to see me."

He nodded slowly, his expression guarded. "Okay."

"He said the first module is supposed to be boring to weed people out. I'd figured out as much for myself. But I think there's an additional reason for the boredom, when it comes to my team and me. I think we're supposed to be doing something. Something we do on our own, without being told. I think it's a test. So I'm looking for the answer." Her words came out slowly at the beginning, but got faster as she spoke.

His words came more deliberately, as if he were weighing each one before he spoke it. "What isn't said is often more important than what is said."

"So there is something, then," she pressed.

"There's always something. It will *always* be something if you go through with Blackout. Your life won't be yours. You'll always be on the edge, waiting for the next thing to land on you."

She sat on the couch. "Are you sorry you joined?"

He sat too. "Everyone regrets it. Not just once. You'll regret it when you have to do things civilized people never do. You'll regret it when you have to do a bad thing for a good reason. You'll regret it when you *don't* regret doing a bad thing because it's become normal to you. You'll regret it when you see other people getting married or just living a normal, peaceful life. Most of all, you'll regret knowing things that most people never have to know. But I wouldn't change it, so no, I'm not sorry."

"Is it forbidden for a Blackout officer to marry?"

He gazed upward slightly, in thought. "It's not forbidden. It just isn't done. Who would I marry? Someone on my team? That would sure narrow the possibilities, even if it wouldn't be dangerous to the team as a whole. But who else could there be for me? We don't have real names. We don't have real identities. Outside of those we work with, nobody knows anything about us but whatever cover identity we're using at the time. Why? Do you have a burning desire for domestic bliss?"

The way he said it made her laugh. "No. I've never even considered it."

Well. She'd never considered the typical idea of marriage. She *had* imagined life with Raptor a time or two. But that was different.

"Well, good. No one but your team will ever see you for who you really are. And your team will know you as well as you know yourself, and who wants to marry someone like that?" He made a comical face of disgust. "Gross."

She smiled. Minho was actually kind of likeable when he wasn't annoying her.

"Why are you really here?" She'd asked him that before, but if she asked again, maybe she'd get a different answer.

"Why are *you* really here?"

She grinned, and he grinned back.

She was kind of starting to like him.

Fallon was thrilled to reach the end of module one. With all the boredom behind her, she could focus on the training mission Admiral Krazinski had mentioned.

She couldn't wait to actually *do* something again. She'd kept up her physical training, both on her own and during practice sessions with Peregrine, Hawk, and Raptor. She ran every morning, lifted weights in the gym, then they took turns trying to beat each other up. Those were usually the best parts of her day. The officer classes themselves, of course, were so boring that her brain felt like it was going into hibernation.

What would the training be? Another mission? A team-building exercise? They only had two weeks, so that limited how far they could travel. Most likely, they'd remain on Earth, but she kept hoping to get her first look at Jamestown—the space station that served as the PAC's headquarters. It was weeks away, though, so she didn't know when she'd get to see it.

What to pack? Krazinski's message had told them where to be and when, but nothing more.

Would it be weird if she took all her weapons?

Yeah. Probably weird.

She packed only her throwing knives. Surely, if anything else was needed, it would be provided. Then she folded some basic clothes, an extra pair of shoes, a couple of infoboards, and her personal hygiene items.

On second thought, she got her bo staff and put it next to the bag. Better safe than sorry.

In that vein, she went to the kitchen and got a box of protein bars. She often ate them after workouts to maintain her muscle mass. She also grabbed a case of hydrating biogel. She liked to drink one after particularly hard workouts to make sure her electrolytes were in balance and she was properly hydrated.

At least she wouldn't have to worry about Hawk stealing those. He hated them.

She took the items back to her room and put them in her bag. She tried to think if she should bring anything else.

Her digital lockpick kit?

Nah. Her skills in that department were nothing compared to

Raptor's. He'd have much better equipment, too. She should see what he planned to bring.

She paused at the door to the necessary. Wait, should she go out into the hall and knock on the regular door? Was it weird to knock on the bathroom door?

Was it weird for her to go to his room at all?

Nothing else in her life had ever brought her so much self-doubt. She'd always been so sure of herself, but when it came to him...he was her weak spot.

She steeled herself. She mentally filled herself with priyanomine. She was hard. Noncombustible. Then she pictured Minho and imagined how he'd handle the situation.

Squaring her shoulders, she stepped through the bathroom and knocked on his door and immediately opened it.

Minho wouldn't have waited for an answer. And if that was what he'd do—and he'd sure never been in a bed with Raptor—then that's what she'd do.

Raptor looked at her, surprised. Like her, he'd put his bag on his bed and appeared to be packing things into it. "Hi."

"Hi." This wasn't awkward. Nope. It was totally normal for two people on a team together. She stepped farther into the room. "Are you bringing any of your gear?"

"I was just trying to decide," he admitted. "What are you bringing?"

"Weapons. Emergency food and biogel. A medkit." She'd just thought of that last one, but she'd add it to her things.

"You think we'll need all that?"

"I don't know. I think we shouldn't assume anything, and we should prepare to fight for our lives."

His forehead crinkled, like it did when he was thinking hard.

He was really cute when he did that.

Immediately, she mentally blasted herself. Would Minho note how cute Raptor looked? She seriously doubted it. So she shouldn't, either.

Nope, he was entirely not cute at all. He was her teammate.

He nodded, looking resolute. "Right. So you've got the weapons. I'll bring the ease-of-entry gear."

"Ease of entry?"

He grinned. "Yeah."

She snorted. Then she laughed. The phrase "ease-of-entry gear" certainly sounded more positive than "breaking-into-places-we-aren't-welcome gear."

"Sounds good." She grinned back at him, and suddenly everything felt terrific. Like they were back at the academy and going on a mission. They were in sync, in tune, and ready to roll.

It felt bloody fantastic.

"You all packed?" he asked.

"Yeah. I'll go check on Hawk and Peregrine."

"Make sure they're bringing their A-game."

She grinned. "All the tricks, right?"

"Blood and bone."

She hadn't heard that since shortly before their graduation. Somehow, things had fragmented since then. Other things had gotten in the way. But they were getting back on track now.

"Blood and bone," she agreed.

She hurried down the hallway to the other side. Since Hawk's room was first, she went there before Peregrine's. She let herself in, not bothering to knock.

He stood in front of his closet, frowning. He glared at her. "I could have been naked!"

She rolled her eyes. "Sorry to disappoint you. But believe me, if you had been, I wouldn't have enjoyed it at all."

He scowled at her. "You really know how to hurt a guy."

She grinned. "I'm taking a census. What are you bringing?"

She nodded toward the bag on his bed.

"Is that the right word? Isn't a census about people? I think you're looking for the word, consensus.'" He looked incredibly pleased with himself.

"Actually, I was invoking an ancient form of the word that's still on the books that involved the valuation of property. But okay. Let's go with your word."

He deflated, and putting a hand to his chest, backed up to sit on his bed. "I thought we were friends."

Grinning, she leaned over him to peer into his bag.

He put a big hand on her face and gently shoved her away. "There are different levels of friends."

"What level are we?"

He screwed his face up into an expression of deep contemplation. "I'd say we're at the level where I'd be willing to take a bite of your sandwich, but would refuse to share my own."

"I think that just kind of paints you as an asshole," she observed.

He grinned. "See? That's where we really are. You don't balk at the idea of me eating your sandwich, and you'll call me a foul name even though I could easily smash you like a bug."

He pinched his forefinger and thumb together to demonstrate.

She considered. "No, you really couldn't, but I like your answer. I'll take it. Seriously, though, what are you bringing? Raptor and I are preparing for anything. We're not going to expect what we need to be provided. Food, weapons, tools, bring it all."

"Ooh, this is starting to sound fun now. If this turns out boring, I'll be pissed."

She turned and sat next to him. "I'm pretty sure that, whatever it is, it won't be boring."

"Good." He flicked her in the forehead with his middle finger. "Go worry about your own shit. I'll handle mine."

"Ow!" She rubbed her forehead. It really hurt. "That's going to leave a big red mark for an hour."

"Yeah." He seemed very pleased by that fact.

She snorted with laughter and left his room.

Instead of barging into Peregrine's room, Fallon carefully knocked.

"Come in."

Fallon poked her head in.

Peregrine sat at the voicecom. Unlike the others, she seemed uninterested in the process of packing.

"I just wanted to check in," Fallon said. "We're all packing for any contingency. Weapons. Rations. Gear. We'll be ready for anything."

Peregrine pushed back from the voicecom display. "For anything." She nodded. "Sounds good. I'll be ready."

Fallon hesitated. She didn't have the closeness with Peregrine that she felt with Hawk and Raptor, but they were working on it. "Can I help you with anything?"

Peregrine paused, then asked, "Would you rather be a blond or a ginger?"

"What? Neither." Then she realized Peregrine was talking about disguises. She must be planning ahead for what to bring. "Uh, ginger, I guess? I mean, that'd be a change of pace, right?"

Peregrine's features softened slightly into her equivalent of a smile. "All right, then."

"Are you excited?" Fallon asked. "I mean, it's hard to tell with you. The rest of us are stoked."

"Stoked?" Peregrine seemed puzzled by the word.

"You know. Pumped up. Energized."

"Oh. Yes. This should be very interesting."

"You don't seem excited," Fallon observed.

"Eh. You know me. I don't show my feelings a lot. But trust me. I'm...stoked?"

"Stoked," Fallon confirmed.

"Right. I'm entirely stoked."

Fallon smiled. Peregrine was trying now, and that was what mattered. They didn't have the ease that Fallon felt with Hawk and Raptor, but they'd get there.

Maybe this training mission would make that happen.

AVIAN UNIT ARRIVED, as ordered, at the coordinates Krazinski had sent them. With no further instruction, and no way to find out precisely what was at those coordinates, all Fallon could do was keep her chin up and hope for the best.

She adjusted her backpack. With the food and biogel inside, it was a bit heavy.

Hawk was the first to speak. "It's an empty field."

"No wonder we couldn't find any designation for this spot," Raptor said.

Fallon slipped her backpack off and set it on the ground. "I guess we wait, then."

"They could have told us to arrive later if no one was going to be here," Hawk complained.

"This is the mission." Fallon sat next to the backpack. "Whatever we need to do, that's what they want us doing."

Peregrine took off her backpack and sat, too. Raptor joined them. Though Hawk took off his backpack, he prowled around restlessly, kicking at rocks and muttering.

Fallon suspected he had a lot of nervous energy and was funneling it into irritation. It didn't bother her.

"How long do you think we'll be waiting here?" Peregrine asked, squinting up at the sunny, almost cloudless sky.

"No telling," Fallon said. "It depends on whether we're actually just waiting for someone to get here, or if waiting is part of the assignment."

"Like the first module?" Raptor grinned.

She smiled back. "More or less."

"Ever think we'll get to a point where they won't screw around with us just to teach us something?" he asked.

"Sure," Hawk said, scratching his ear. "Somewhere along

the way, we'll need to be fully functional and autonomous. That's when they'll stop wasting their time screwing around with us."

Raptor smiled. "That's very pragmatic thinking, Hawk."

Hawk gazed out into the distance. "I'm a very pragmatic guy."

Fallon sat up straighter. "Do you hear that?"

She tilted her head, trying to better hear the faint sound.

"I think I hear something." Peregrine looked uncertain.

"Probably just a commuter plane in the distance," Hawk said.

"I don't think so." She kept listening.

"Yeah," Raptor said. "I hear it now."

She shielded her eyes with her hand and gazed up at the sky, but didn't see so much as a speck. She wasn't sure which direction to look, either. In such a wide open space, acoustics could be misleading.

"There." Peregrine pointed.

Squinting, Fallon thought she spotted a dark dot. It could have been a large bird, maybe, but she didn't think so.

They waited in silence, watching as it grew from a speck to a blob. Then from a blob to the definite shape of a ship. The sound gradually grew louder too.

"That's coming here, isn't it?" Hawk stared out at it.

Raptor said, "I'm pretty sure that whatever we're here for, it starts with that ship."

"It's an atmosphere-only ship," Fallon said. "So we're not leaving the planet. At least not yet, anyway."

"You can tell that by looking?" Hawk glanced at her.

"Sure. I recognize the model. Sturdy craft, good repair record, often used for steep ascents."

"Not sure I love the sound of that." Hawk frowned.

They watched the ship approach, then hover, before slowly lowering itself to the ground.

"Think we should walk over?" Raptor asked.

Fallon shook her head. "Our orders said to be at these coordinates. We're right on them. We'll follow those orders to the letter unless we have an excellent reason not to."

The back hatch of the vessel opened, and a ramp eased into place. A single figure walked down it.

The four of them watched as the person approached them with an unhurried gait. When he stood directly in front of them, Fallon raised her eyebrows and remained sitting. She'd let him speak first.

"Hello, cadets. My name's Minho, and I'll be delivering your orders today."

Hawk put his hands in his pockets. "I'll take a double-decker sandwich and a side of macaroni salad."

Minho grinned. "Not that kind of order."

Finally, Fallon stood, casually dusting off her pants. "What are we supposed to do, then?"

Minho reached into a pocket and handed her a small infoboard. "All you have to do is reach those coordinates, by any means at your disposal."

"That sounds too easy." Hawk crowded close to her. "What's the catch?"

"Well, that particular location isn't exactly easily accessible, and it tends to be a wee bit hostile to random people showing up unannounced."

"How about we announce ourselves, then?" Hawk's question was more brash wiseassery than it was an actual question.

"Bad idea, since it's a stealth mission. But then sometimes bad ideas are good ideas, so I guess we'll see." Minho grinned, as if pleased with himself for adding an extra degree of enigma to his message.

"So you aren't coming with us?" Fallon asked.

"Nope."

"Is there anyone else on that ship?"

"Nope. But I've heard you're a decent pilot." Minho smiled.

"Anything else we ought to know?" Peregrine approached, looking wary.

"No. Just get there. Starting with that." Minho pointed at the ship. "Simple, right?"

Fallon answered, "I seriously doubt that whatever this is will turn out to be simple."

"Probably a good instinct," Minho agreed. "Good luck!"

Minho began walking away from them. Where he was going, Fallon didn't know. Probably a drop site where a vehicle would pick him up. At the moment, though, he seemed to be wandering toward the middle of nowhere.

Actually, no, they were already in the middle of nowhere.

"Should we stop him?' Raptor wore a puzzled frown as he watched Minho.

Hawk grabbed his backpack and started walking toward the ship. "Why bother? He said what he had to say. Let's go."

The others followed.

When they got to the ship, Hawk stepped back and gestured to Fallon. "You go first."

"Why?"

"Because you're familiar with the model. And also, to spring any booby traps."

She smiled. "Right."

She slid her backpack half off and reached inside the long, skinny side pocket. She pulled out two long, thin pieces of polished synthwood.

"What's that?" Hawk asked.

Instead of saying it, she demonstrated it. She fitted the pieces together at the ends, pushed, twisted, then pulled again.

"Tada. Travel bo staff." She flourished it over her head, then set one end on the deck plate in front of her.

"Handy," Hawk said. "Now go."

She crept forward through the loading bay, holding her stick ready. She could use it to smack an obstacle out of the way or defend herself, should either be necessary. There was always the chance Krazinski would test them in some way.

But nothing jumped out to threaten them as she led them through the ship and up to the bridge.

Which left her standing on the small bridge, holding a big stick and feeling a little silly.

"Well, then." She wrenched the staff to break it into two parts again, and shoved them and her backpack at Hawk. "Take care of these."

"What, why?" Hawk looked a little annoyed.

"Because I need to fly this bird. Unless you want to."

"Oh." Hawk accepted the items. "As long as there's a good reason."

Fallon looked to Peregrine. "Do you know how to fly?"

Peregrine shook her head.

"Take the co-pilot's seat. I'll show you some basics." Fallon sat at the helm.

"Yeah?"

Fallon glanced over at Peregrine. Did she look a little bit pleased?

Fallon suspected she did. "Yeah."

"What, I don't get to learn?" Raptor joked.

"You'll all need to learn some basics. You two can have a seat and listen in."

She took them through typical pre-flight checks for an atmospheric takeoff on a PAC planet. Safety checks, mechanical checks, takeoff checks, and checking in with flight control—which, of course, in this case didn't apply.

"That's a lot of checks," Hawk remarked.

"Flight is dangerous. The fuel and the equipment used to achieve flight are dangerous. Checks aren't sexy, but they can prevent a person from getting their head incinerated by an exhaust port."

Hawk's voice came from behind her, sounding grim. "Yeah, let's avoid that."

She smirked. "Okay. Here we go."

Instead of a rolling start to gain enough velocity to take flight, this sweet ship had vertical thrusters to take them straight up.

Should she give them a quick ascent so they could feel that delightful dip in their stomachs?

She imagined Hawk's response. There would be much swearing involved, she was certain.

Nah, not today. She'd save that for another time.

She fired the thrusters and they gently buoyed upward. Watching their altitude, she made sure they ascended at a gentle, constant rate.

"There we are. Now forward. It'll take us about two hours to get there."

"I wonder what happens then," Raptor mused.

"We'll see," Peregrine said. "And then we'll get the job done."

"Yeah, we will," Hawk agreed. "Blood and bone."

Fallon smiled. She had a good feeling about this mission.

6

Two hours later, when Fallon got a good look at their destination, she didn't have such a good feeling.

She'd taken an aerial survey, since the voicecom indicated that this was classified land owned by PAC command and accessible only to people who had clearance.

No doubt they'd chosen the location carefully, given its generally inhospitable conditions.

Located in the center of a half-collapsed mountaintop, the entire area was rockslides, precarious ledges, and steep drops.

There was no putting a ship down there, even with vertical thrusters. Even a lightweight helicopter would have a difficult time finding a secure touchdown spot.

She pulled a lever under her seat to allow her to turn and look at her teammates. News like this had to be delivered face-to-face.

"Okay, I've got some bad news."

Hawk and Raptor frowned while Peregrine simply looked at her.

"There's no place to land down there."

Blood and Bone 73

"So...what? We find the nearest spot and hike in?" Hawk asked.

"It would be rough. First of all, we'd have to be very far out, and hiking over this terrain would be treacherous. This place is a structural nightmare. We'd all likely end up with broken legs, if not necks. And besides that, taking this bird down there would create downdrafts and vibrations that could cause a major rockslide."

"There's got to be a way in," Raptor said. "We've been ordered to get there. They wouldn't give us an impossible task, would they?"

"They might," Peregrine said. "Just to see how we handle it."

Fallon nodded. "Yeah, I could see that. But there is a way in. You're just not going to like it."

Hawk's eyes narrowed. "Why?"

"Have you ever jumped out of a plane?"

He shook his head. "No. Never been in one that was about to crash."

"I mean like skydiving."

"Jump out of a perfectly good plane? Do I look stupid?"

Raptor grinned. "Well, I wasn't going to say anything before, but..."

Hawk scowled. "Watch it, preppy boy."

"It'll be fine. I'll show you how," Fallon promised.

"You've skydived before?" Hawk looked doubtful.

"Numerous times. It's part of the flight training program at the academy. I'd done it before the academy, too."

He stared at her. "You're just mentioning this now?"

Fallon shrugged. "Do I know everything about you there is to know?"

He sighed. "You're serious about this jumping out thing, aren't you? You're not just teasing me?"

He sounded hopeful.

"Nope. We're definitely going out. That's what they wanted,

and that's what we're going to do. I'm circling us around to a suitable drop zone."

"What about the ship?" Peregrine asked.

"I've programmed the autopilot to take it to the nearest airfield. It'll be fine." Fallon turned around and checked their progress.

"Okay!" She stood. "Let's get suited up."

"Are you sure there's equipment for this?" Hawk asked.

"Yep. Safety pre-flight requires a manifest check to make sure appropriate evacuation supplies are available."

Hawk sighed and stood, looking resigned. "Fine. Let's hurry up and do it so it can be over with sooner."

"That's the spirit." Raptor patted him on the shoulder.

Hawk slanted a dangerous look his way, but Raptor only grinned. He knew Hawk wasn't really threatening him. It was just how Hawk reacted to certain kinds of stress.

In the loading bay, Fallon pulled open a storage locker. "Right. Extra large, that's for you."

She pointed at Hawk, then to the locker. She pulled one out for Peregrine. "You could use medium or large, as they adjust a great deal, so here."

"Same goes for me, I guess?" Raptor asked.

"Probably, but go with large, since you have such wide shoulders." She grabbed a size small and hoped no one cracked a joke about her size.

She showed them how to put them on. "Make sure all the parts are adjusted right. Too loose, and you'll have a dangerous amount of play. Too tight, and you could break something when the parachute snaps you back. All the pieces are there to ease the jolt and distribute the pressure as you descend."

She put on her own suit and gear, then one by one, checked her teammates. She started with their feet, worked up to the harnesses on their thighs, and kept going.

As she ran her fingers over Hawk's chest, he said, "I kinda feel like you're copping a feel, here."

She smirked at him. "I'm checking your suit for holes, rips, or snags."

"Yeah you are."

She flicked him in the forehead, just as he'd so recently done to her.

"Ow." He grumbled.

"Peregrine, can you double-check my suit?" she asked.

Peregrine looked it over, then said, "I don't see anything wrong with it."

"Good. Okay. Here's the rundown. You don't have much to worry about. We're at a relatively low altitude, so you'll be able to breathe just fine. Since we'll have no masks on, we'll have no communication. So keep an eye on one another. Don't get too close, or you can get tangled lines. I'll let you know when to go, then I'll jump last."

She demonstrated how to lean out and fall belly-down, arms and legs bent. Then she demonstrated how to crumple and roll on landing.

"The suits do the hard work. They'll autodeploy the 'chutes at the right altitude, and they'll direct you to the desired coordinates. They'll absorb a lot of the wind shear, and they'll even absorb some of the shock of landing. Just try to relax and enjoy the flight."

Raptor grinned at her, but Hawk grimaced.

"Enjoy?" Hawk repeated. "I don't think so. Maybe you like trusting your life to some machinery, but I don't."

"I could make the jump without the suit. It just makes it easier and safer. People have been doing this for centuries, just for fun."

"What about our backpacks?" Raptor asked. "We can't wear them with 'chutes on our backs. Do we just leave our gear behind?"

"I'm glad you asked." Fallon opened another storage locker and unstrapped a large piece of equipment. "This is a follow-drone. It will follow whoever's wearing this."

She activated the unit, making it come alive with lights and a slight hum, then detached a rubbery circlet from it. She showed them the bracelet, then put it around her wrist and pulled her suit down over it.

She opened the follow-drone's claws, attaching her backpack straps to them. She indicated that the others should do the same, then closed the drone's clamps.

"All set! Any questions?"

"Uh," Raptor said, "Who goes first?"

Peregrine said, "I will."

Fallon admired her fiercely at that moment. She was certain Peregrine had never done this, but she didn't show an ounce of worry. She just stood there, strong and stoic.

It was darn cool, and made Fallon proud to be her teammate.

"I guess I'll go second," Raptor said.

"Good. If there's nothing else, I'll open up the door." She looked from face to face. "Remember, just lean down into the wind and let yourself tip forward. Don't jump or do anything dramatic. You don't want to be spinning around. Trust the equipment to do its job, and I'll see you on the ground."

Peregrine nodded, her jaw set in a determined expression. Raptor nodded, looking somewhat less sure. Hawk simply scowled.

"Over here. I'll close the internal door to keep it from interfering with the ship. We don't want it to think it's experiencing a hull breach or something."

She closed the door, which put them in a small, confined space lit by emergency lights. Before opening the exterior door, she looked at the three faces with her, lit with a neon backglow.

She put her hand out. "Blood and bone."

Raptor put his hands on hers. "Blood and bone."

Peregrine put her hand on Raptor's. "Blood and bone."

Hawk sighed and slapped his big hand on top. "Blood and bone. Dammit."

Fallon grinned. She opened the door. Immediately, rough wind buffeted them, but it quickly equaled out. The noise remained tremendous, overwhelming all other sounds.

Fallon put her hand on Peregrine's shoulder. This woman, this teammate of hers, was about to be the first to leap off a plane on nothing but Fallon's instruction.

For a moment, she was struck with awe, humility, and a split second of terror for having been bestowed that kind of trust and responsibility for someone else.

Then she stepped closer to the edge, with Peregrine going with her.

Fallon squeezed her shoulder and leaned close to her ear. "Go!"

Peregrine didn't hesitate. She leaned out, extending her body just as Fallon had said, and fell into the sky.

Raptor stepped out. She put her hand on his shoulder, looking down at the swiftly shrinking outline of Peregrine. She squeezed his shoulder. "Go!"

Hawk's eyes were wider than she'd ever seen them. She reached her hand out to him. He took it and moved closer.

She stepped into his chest and put her lips against his ear. "You're going to do great. I'm right behind you."

He gave her a quick, tight hug that took her breath, then nodded and stepped to the edge.

She squeezed his shoulder. "Go!"

He let himself fall out of the plane, rapidly descending after the others.

She counted out a safe interval between them, then shuffled her feet to the edge and pointed her heart toward Earth.

She fell.

She was weightless. Untethered. The wind battered her face

in a not painful, but very distracting way. Her stomach was alive with the thrill of butterflies.

Her blood was full of lightning.

Somewhere behind her, the follow-drone would be pursuing. She hoped nothing happened to it, since it held all their food and basic supplies.

All too soon, the parachute deployed, slowing her descent. The thrill ride became more of a gentle float downward.

At least, until the ground got closer. Once it solidified in her view, it suddenly seemed to rush upward at her.

She braced, making her ankles and knees soft, preparing for impact. She hit and rolled, and her 'chute billowed over her in a big, gray poof before quickly settling.

She unstrapped her parachute pack and hurried out from under.

Raptor and Peregrine stood, grinning.

Well, he was grinning. She had a slight smile. But on her, it looked like a grin.

"Wait. Where's Hawk?"

Raptor pointed upward.

She looked up to see a rapidly descending hulk of man.

A faint sound reached her ears and grew. It was a steady, enthusiastic scream.

The scream got louder, the hulk got bigger, then he hit the ground in a billow of parachute and prolific swear words.

"Guess he caught an updraft," Fallon said. "How was it?"

Raptor grinned even bigger. "About two seconds after I landed, I decided it was crazy fun."

"Loser," Peregrine said. "I decided that two seconds *before* I landed."

Hopped up on the thrill of adrenaline, they laughed together.

A laugh from Peregrine! Fallon would have to mark it on the calendar.

She grasped the edge of Hawk's chute and peered under. "You alive under there?"

Hawk came out, still wearing his pack and dragging the parachute around. She helped him take it off.

"Yeah. Alive," he grunted.

"You sure were screaming," Raptor observed.

"I wasn't screaming," Hawk denied. "You were screaming."

"Uh, right," Raptor said, not sounding convinced. "I forgot. That was me."

The follow-drone arrived, setting down a few meters away from Fallon.

"Grab your backpacks," she said. "We should get going."

Two hours into their hike, the thrill of skydiving had worn off, and the difficulty of traveling over rough terrain had sunk in.

Hawk led the way, not because he had special skills in being a trail guide, but because it ensured he, as the largest, had enough room to get through. Peregrine followed behind him so they could help each other if they stumbled or got stuck.

Fallon went next, with Raptor behind her.

It was slow going. Each step had to be tested before shifting weight, and more than once, one of them had taken a dangerous slide before being caught by the arm.

As daylight faded into dusk, Fallon realized they weren't going to make it in time.

"We're going to have to camp out," she said during a brief rest. "We can't keep going much longer. We'll break our necks."

"It's going to cool off a lot when the sun goes down, and we don't have tents," Hawk observed.

"I don't suppose any of you are wilderness survival experts, are you?" Fallon asked, finding the possibility extremely unlikely.

Hawk sighed. "Let's find a place with flat ground, where we aren't likely to turn over in our sleep and roll down a hill."

Did that mean he was a wilderness survival expert? Or that he just figured, however much he knew, it had to be more than the rest of them?

She'd wait it out and see which it looked like.

By the time the sun approached the horizon, they'd found a decent spot. The ground was relatively flat for several meters, and no large animals seemed to be living nearby.

Hawk dropped his backpack on the ground. "The good news is that where we are, wind isn't going to bother us, and it doesn't look likely we'll get rain. Bad news is that the temperature's going to drop quite a bit."

Fallon could already feel a difference on her face and hands. "The suits will help, but not for the exposed parts of our skin."

Hawk nodded. "We can build a lean-to and a fire pit, and that should keep us warm enough. Where are we on food and water?"

"I've got enough protein bars and biogel for us all, for a couple days," Fallon said.

"I brought some stuff," Raptor added.

"Me too," Peregrine added.

"So did I. Good." Hawk seemed satisfied. "I don't suppose anyone brought blankets or pillows, though."

Silence.

Fallon said, "I could send the follow-drone back to grab the parachutes."

"You could do that?" Hawk asked.

"Sure. It can't do all that on its own, but I'm a great drone pilot."

Hawk shrugged. "How fast can it go?"

"Should be pretty fast. We haven't actually gone very far, since it's such rough going."

She went to the follow-drone and programmed it with the

coordinates of their drop. "When it gets there, I'll pick up the 'chutes and have it return."

The drone took off.

"How much battery does that thing have?" Peregrine asked.

"It'll make it there and back, but then it will be done until the sun comes out again. It does well on solar but sucks up reserve battery really fast."

"Okay. Let's work on the lean-to frame while we wait."

When the follow-drone arrived back at the drop zone, Fallon sat down and put on a pair of goggles. She connected them and a small remote and sat down.

Her vision became that of the drone. She saw everything it did, and nothing else. Operating its claw clamps was difficult, because it really wasn't meant for this kind of use. Eventually, she managed to hover at just the right height and angle, and move forward just enough to hook each of the packs. Then she increased the drone's altitude to keep the deployed 'chutes from dragging the ground.

She flew the drone back, doing her best not to let the 'chutes get tangled in a tree. It took longer than expected. The low battery warning started blinking.

Clenching the control, she tried to hurry, but not hurry so much as to be reckless.

Finally, she got it back, and lowered it to the ground slowly, alongside the packs and 'chutes.

She sighed with relief.

Hawk patted her on the head. "Good job."

She should feel condescended to, but secretly, his rare praise made her feel all warm and gooey inside.

She'd never tell him that, though.

Hawk and Peregrine covered the lean-to with one of the 'chutes, leaving it attached to the pack to anchor it down. They cut the other three 'chutes loose of their packs, which took some work.

Fallon and Raptor gathered rocks and made a stone circle, then filled the circle with deadfall. Then they added smaller sticks and branches for kindling.

"Uh," Fallon said, "you brought a lighter, right?"

Hawk scoffed. "Of course I did."

He rummaged around in his backpack. After several minutes he sighed and straightened. "That is, I meant to."

Fallon groaned.

Raptor laughed. He went to his own pack and held out a lighter to Hawk. "Here."

"Not bad, preppy boy."

"Says the hairy man-beast," Peregrine muttered under her breath.

Surprised, Fallon laughed.

"What was that?" Hawk bent to light the kindling. "Something about hairy feet?"

"Hairy man-beast," Fallon repeated, enunciating each syllable carefully, and rather enjoying it. "It's what we call you behind your back when you eat all the food."

"That right?" Hawk didn't seem perturbed. "I kind of like it. It sounds...manly. And forbidding."

She tossed him a couple of protein bars and a pouch of biogel. "Here."

He looked at the food. "You're a lousy cook. You're fired."

"I don't see you handing it back," she retorted.

He grabbed his backpack then handed a flat packet to Raptor on his left. He made a *pass it around* motion.

When they all had a packet, Hawk passed around pouches of water. Real water, not biogel, which was thicker and had a distinctive tangy taste.

Fallon tried to read the words on her packet by firelight. It wasn't easy. "Is this...reconstituted Bennite stew?"

"Not yet." Hawk connected the pouches and squeezed water into the food pouch. "But it's about to be."

He gave the pouch a gentle shake, then set it close to the fire. "Give it a few minutes and it will even get warm."

They all followed suit.

"I've changed my opinion of you," Raptor declared.

"From what to what?" Hawk squinted at him with a faux-dangerous glare.

"From nearly useless to only somewhat useless." Raptor grinned.

Hawk laughed.

They opened their pouches and Fallon was surprised to discover that it was pretty good. It was too fine and smooth, of course, as if someone had pre-chewed it, but the flavor was quite tasty.

After that, they moved on to the protein bars and the dried fruit Peregrine had brought.

All in all, it wasn't a bad meal.

After they'd eaten, they gazed into the flames, which had grown to a respectably decent little blaze.

Hawk said, "It's going to be a boring night, isn't it?"

"I've had livelier ones," Raptor said. "But way worse ones too. How about you do something to liven things up?"

"Like what?"

"Wrestle a bear or something."

"There are no bears around here."

Raptor looked disappointed. "You sure?"

"Pretty sure."

"Crocodile?" Raptor suggested.

"Yeah, no. Definitely no crocodiles on this continent. At least not in the wild." Hawk threw him a look of disgust.

"Okay. How about two really angry raccoons?"

Fallon burst out laughing. "Yes, please. That would be something to see."

"You think I can't beat a couple of furballs?" Hawk pretended offense.

"I dunno," Fallon answered. "Those raccoons can get really pissy."

Hawk laughed

They watched the fire for several long minutes.

"Do you think this is what it's like?" Peregrine asked. "Doing missions?"

Peregrine didn't speak up a lot, and she sure didn't ask questions often, so Fallon considered her answer carefully.

"Only sort of. I think missions will always be strange things we didn't expect or have never done, and we just have to figure stuff out as we go along. Find solutions. You know?"

"So, sort of like this, but also never like this." Peregrine nodded slowly.

"Yeah, I guess so."

The sky had gone dark and they had eaten, so sleep seemed the next logical step.

"Anyone tired?" Fallon asked.

A trio of "no" replies came in response.

"Yeah. Me neither. What to do? It's not like we can just spin up a holo-vid or something."

"What did people used to do at campfires, before holo-vids?" Raptor asked.

"I don't know," Hawk said. "Hide from dinosaurs?"

They laughed.

"Seriously, though," Raptor said, "you know that dinosaurs died out way before people existed, right?"

Hawk shrugged. "Before humans existed, sure. But can you really be sure no alien species from the next galaxy never visited here and were like, *holy scrap, what is that?* when they saw a giant lizard-monster?"

"Maybe," Peregrine said thoughtfully, "the aliens were giant lizard-monsters, too, so it just looked normal to them."

"Deep thoughts, man," Hawk said. "Deep thoughts."

They all laughed. Even Peregrine let out a small chuckle.

"Do any of you sing or something?" Raptor asked when they quieted down again. "Seems likely that people sat by the campfire and entertained each other with stories or songs."

Fallon, Hawk, and Peregrine shook their heads.

"No singers, huh?" Raptor sighed. "You'd think Blackout could have assigned us a fifth member as a jester or bard or something."

"Pretty sure that would make us more of a comedy spoof than an elite covert task force," Fallon said.

Hawk shrugged. "At least we'd be entertained."

"I could get my throwing knives and we can all take turns being 'it.'" Fallon joked.

"I'd need to be pretty drunk to agree to that," Hawk said.

Peregrine tossed a stick into the fire. "Being drunk would ensure that you lost."

"But I'd have fun, so win some, lose some." Hawk grinned.

Fallon shifted on the hard ground. "So you'd get drunk and have a knife-flinging melee for laughs, but you were worried about a little skydiving?"

He shrugged. "I'd never done it before. I'm sure next time will be better. I just don't really like heights."

Fallon blinked at him. "Don't like heights?" She pointed up at the sky. "You realize we're likely to spend a great deal of our careers up in space, right?"

"Entirely different," he insisted. "Height only exists within an atmosphere. In deep space, it's not about height or depth, but about a reduced zone you can survive in."

Fallon opened her mouth, but found she had no counterargument. "Huh. That...actually makes sense."

"You sound surprised."

"I expected you to say something goofy again," Fallon admitted.

In the darkness, she could see Raptor and Peregrine nodding in agreement.

Hawk raised his arms up over his head and stretched. "Since we don't have any booze, or enough food to pig out, I guess I'll try to sleep. We'll want to be moving as soon as it's light. Otherwise we're just sitting targets."

Raptor looked toward him. "You think they're hunting us?"

"I don't know that they're not. So shouldn't we assume that they might be? But unless they were using drones, they're not going to be able to approach us here without us hearing them coming. So we should be fine to sleep without taking guard shifts."

Fallon liked that he was thinking about all that. "I guess we should try to sleep, though I'm so keyed up I'm not sure I'll be able to."

"Fresh air's good for falling asleep," Peregrine said. "Just try lying down and closing your eyes. Fatigue should set in."

Hawk moved forward to the fire. "I'll show you how to bank a fire so it's low but steady. With our 'chutes as covers, we'll be plenty warm."

Once they'd done that and sealed up all the food and food wrappers to avoid attracting wildlife, they grabbed the parachutes and improvised some bedding. They used one for some padding underneath, and folded up the top to form a long pillow for them all. Then Peregrine and Hawk shared one 'chute as a blanket, while Fallon and Raptor used the remaining one. They'd tried cutting them into smaller pieces, but the material was too durable for the inadequate tools they had.

They lay down about half a meter apart, all in a row. Fallon put her head on the makeshift pillow and turned to her side.

She heard nature sounds. Bugs, probably, and maybe some owls or other nocturnal birds. She should probably start learning about wildlife on various planets, starting with Earth. She could look it up on an infoboard, but she might not always have an infoboard, and her life could conceivably depend on knowing how to survive in the elements.

She had a lot to learn.

She felt a hand on her shoulder. Since she was looking at Hawk's back, it had to be Raptor's hand.

Was he reassuring her? Looking for reassurance? Just making sure she had enough 'chute on her side?

She lifted her hand and rested it on his. After a gentle squeeze, she let go and his hand moved away.

Lying in the dark, with her team next to her, she listened to her surroundings. She heard no footfalls, no whispers, and no approaching wildlife.

She closed her eyes.

FALLON GLANCED at her comport again. The distance between the team and the assigned coordinates was shrinking fast. They'd make it there within the hour.

Hawk led. Sometimes that meant doubling back when a ledge crumbled when he tested it. They'd had to find alternate routes several times, which meant it had taken them four hours to cover two kilometers.

But they'd made it. Two hundred meters. A hundred. Fifty. They were directly on top of it.

The only problem was the y-axis. Wherever they were meant to arrive was fifty meters straight down.

There had to be a way down the cliffside. Or something.

With her forehead streaked with dirt and sweat, and her lungs full of dust, Fallon was more than ready to arrive at their destination and declare victory.

Hawk threw an arm out behind him, stopping in his tracks. "Whoa. Yeah, let's back up."

Cautiously, Fallon peered around his arm.

A steep drop down a cliff face had been hidden by a thick tree line that went right up to the edge. Hawk could have stepped right over into nothing.

They all scooted back from the ledge, just in case the ground beneath their feet decided to shift.

"Okay, who was in charge of the rappelling equipment?" Raptor joked.

"Do you know how to rappel?" Peregrine asked.

"No. Do you?"

She shook her head.

Fallon shrugged and Hawk also shook his head.

"Right, so none of us would know how even if he had the gear," Raptor said.

"So," Hawk said. "What, do we tunnel down through the rock or something? I don't get it."

Fallon retrieved the remote for the follow-drone and had it drop the gear it was carrying. Then she directed it over the ledge. With the goggles on, she saw everything it did.

"There it is," she said. Three meters under their feet, there was a cliff-face opening. "It's a cavern."

"How do we get to it?" Peregrine asked.

Fallon brought the follow-drone back to hover nearby. She removed the goggles. "There's a way."

She looked at the drone pointedly.

Hawk shook his head. "Nuh uh, I'm not dangling from that thing. Did you see that drop? That's a hundred meters straight down a sheer cliff face with no ledges."

"You're too heavy for this little drone," Fallon said. "I'm the only one it can safely carry."

"Safely?" Raptor repeated.

"Relatively speaking." Fallon smiled faintly. "I have good grip strength."

"I don't like it," Peregrine said. "There must be another way."

"I'm open to suggestions." Fallon didn't love her idea, either. She just didn't see an alternative.

No one said anything.

"Right." Fallon nodded resolutely. "I'll have to hang underneath it to avoid the blades. That means my hands won't be free to fly it. Which one of you has the steadiest hands?"

"Me." Peregrine stepped forward. "I've spent years working with tiny components that can short out if you touch another surface just a millimeter away. I'll do it."

Fallon handed her the control. "Okay. Ever used one of these before?"

Peregrine shook her head.

Fallon suppressed a frustrated laugh. Drone piloting wasn't something you learned in five minutes. "Okay. I'm going to measure the flight and program in a steady progression. All you'll really need to do is keep your hands on the controls and listen for me to yell any corrections to you."

Peregrine nodded, looking determined.

Fallon carefully flew the drone back over the intended flight path, marking the coordinates every centimeter of the way. Then she created a program to take the drone on a steady path.

"Just no sudden movements, okay?" she warned. "It'll throw me right off, straight down into the gorge."

"So what you're saying," Peregrine said, grim-faced, "is that if I ever wanted my chance to be leader, this is it."

Fallon blinked. Peregrine delivered the line like it was entirely serious, which made the joke all the funnier.

She laughed. "I'll just have to hope your ambition doesn't outweigh my usefulness. Let's do this before I change my mind."

She handed the remote to Peregrine. "Just keep it still until I have a good grip. Once I'm in there, you can use the drone to see what's happening. We can talk via comport if we need to. Once I'm down, switch the control to auto-follow. Space could be tight in there, and it will do better on its own systems."

"Wait." Raptor spoke suddenly.

They all looked at him and he shook his head. "No. Never mind. Ignore me."

Fallon reached up where the drone hovered and wrapped her hands securely around two of the arms that had secured their gear. She pulled her weight up off the ground and kept her elbows bent to help support herself.

"Go!"

The drone moved. Though the initial movement was slow and gentle, it still rocked her slightly.

Her grip was still good.

Don't look down. Don't look down.

The drone moved over the edge and her feet dangled in open air.

She looked down.

She lost her breath.

There was a difference between jumping out a plane knowing she was wearing a parachute and hanging off a drone with only her grip to save her.

She literally had her life in her own hands.

Redirecting her attention, she resolutely focused on her descent. She drifted gently downward. She could see geological striations on the rock face.

One meter down. Her grip remained strong.

Two meters down. This was fine.

Three meters down. There it was.

The drone moved toward the opening. She hoped nobody would jump out of it at her.

She had to pull her knees up to her chest to clear the ledge, but she was finally able to release her grip and drop to the stone floor.

She'd made it.

With a small wave at the drone to assure the others she was fine, she advanced into the cavern. The rock under her feet was smooth and even with a slight incline. Probably the result of water over a very long period of time. The air was good. Cool and clean. Wasn't there something about some caves having noxious fumes? Or maybe she'd have to get farther underground for that to happen.

She'd have to read up on it later, in case something like this came up again.

The passage narrowed, then widened into a natural rotunda carved out of stone. It also plunged into utter darkness.

Well, that was no good. She couldn't go stumbling around blindly in a cave. She waved at the drone, covered her eyes with her hands, then pointed at the drone.

She hoped they'd understand.

The drone's lights brightened.

"Yes!" She gave the machine a thumbs-up.

Edging into the rotunda, she saw nothing unusual. No sign of habitation, and no clue about what she was supposed to do there.

A steep stone ramp led upward, and she had to walk carefully to keep traction on the smooth stone. Even so, her foot slipped and she fell to her knees. That was probably better. She edged forward on hands and knees to make sure she didn't fall all the way down the steep grade.

If she got seriously injured, there'd be no one to help her out of here.

Right.

A gentle, cold wind blew over her.

Wait, could a cave have wind? She searched her memory but came up with nothing.

She heard something. Dripping. Water.

Following the sound, with the drone behind and above her shoulder, the stone beneath her feet leveled out again, and the narrow passage opened wide.

Another big, rounded opening. She followed the dripping sound and noticed that while the floor was even, it sloped downward. On the far side of the room, she saw where the water was dripping down from a small hole in the ceiling above. The sound bounced off the hard surfaces. Edging around a massive boulder that blocked her path, she looked to see where the water was going.

She pulled in a deep breath. It was a pool. She could walk down right into it. How deep was it?

She either had to go through the water or look for another passageway.

Grabbing her comport from her belt, she checked the destination coordinates. She was almost there. This time, she wasn't above them, but nearly right at the exact location.

Shit.

What was in that water? What was under it?

Could cave water be toxic?

She blew out a breath. She was sadly ignorant about caves.

Her orders had been clear, though. Get to those coordinates, however she could.

She couldn't fly the drone herself, and even with her comport she wouldn't be able to communicate directions fast enough for Peregrine to manage—even if Peregrine could have maneuvered in such tight confines.

Resolutely, she stepped into the water. Within a few steps, she was knee-deep. A few more and she was waist deep.

The cold of the water shot ice through her veins and made her breath come in gasps.

How long did it take for hypothermia to set in?

She didn't know that, either, except that it wasn't long.

It hurt. The cold made her body ache, but at least the water didn't rise above her neck. She doubted she'd have been able to swim well. Her muscles were cramping.

She pulled out the comport and checked it.

One small shift, and she was again hovering directly over the target. This time, though, only three meters separated her and her goal.

Shit shit shit.

She blew out a few breaths and pulled in the deepest lungful she could, then let her knees buckle and plunge her into the freezing blackness. She settled at the bottom of the pool.

Searching with fingers going stiff and numb, she dragged her hands over the stone beneath her. Wait. That wasn't stone. Stone didn't feel like that.

She stood, breaking the surface of the water, and dragged in a fresh lungful of breath before plunging below again. She started scooting backward on her heels to cover more space before she needed another breath, but her lungs grew tight and she started to feel desperate.

Another breath, and down again. She hoped she wasn't feeling the same area over and over again. She was operating blindly.

Just as she was about to stand so she could get another breath, she felt something. A handle.

A handle?

She grabbed it, twisted, and when pulling didn't do anything, she pushed.

A door swung open, dumping her, wet and gasping, onto something hard. Light nearly blinded her, and icy water rushed down over her until it abruptly stopped.

Water dripped, she gasped for breath, and her eyes adjusted.

Fallon shoved her wet hair out of her eyes.

Admiral Krazinski stood on the other side of the room.

Room? Yes. This looked like a PAC building. And the admiral stood there in his uniform, while a couple of commanders stood behind her, resealing the hatch she'd opened.

She wanted answers, but all she could do was shiver violently, her muscles cramping and aching.

"Congratulations, Fallon. You're only the fourth one to ever make it here. Well done. Go get warm and dry, then we'll talk."

She tried to argue. The follow-drone would still be in the cave above, and her team would have no idea that she wasn't currently drowning.

Her lips felt like rubber and her knees wouldn't work. A commander scooped her up and hurried her away.

As they went, she forced her tongue to the back of her teeth. All she needed was one word.

"Team," she got out. The *m* sound was more like a soft *n*, but close enough.

"We'll get them, cadet. You did well. Now just rest for a little bit."

FALLON WAS SITTING ALONE in an office, sipping tea when her team arrived. It took some time, since they had to be driven back down the mountain and in through a hidden tunnel.

That worked out fine, because she'd needed some time under warming blankets to feel functional again.

It was amazing what some cold water could do in mere minutes.

Hawk shouldered his way in ahead of the others, looking like he wanted to fight. When he saw her, he relaxed, then brightened. He strode across the room, picked her up out of her chair and swung her around.

"Yes! We did it!"

She laughed. "We did."

Raptor grinned and even Peregrine looked pleased, in her way. They high-fived each other and exchanged numerous hugs, shouts, and cheers.

"I thought you'd drowned!" Hawk shouted, sounding oddly jubilant about it.

"When the others showed up on that mountain," Peregrine said, "Hawk just about punched their lights out before they could tell him you were fine."

Fallon laughed. "Well, I am. And you know what else?"

They looked at her expectantly.

"Krazinski's here. He said we're only the fourth team ever to make it all the way in."

More whoops and celebrating.

"Oh, and you know what else?" she added.

They were ready for more good news.

"That water was cold as hell, and someone else gets to do that part next time," she declared.

More laughter.

"Hang on," Raptor said. "What's this you're wearing?"

She stepped back and modeled the uniform. It wasn't just a cadet's uniform. It was a full-fledged officer's uniform. Black with a tiny bit of blue trim looked especially good on her, she thought.

"That's the last bit of news," she said. "We're officially officers now. Maybe I should have waited and let the admiral tell you that, but I'm too excited."

"Wait, what?" Peregrine's brow furrowed. "So...where do we go from here?"

"Back to the academy," Fallon said. "But we'll be assuming our old identities as covers. In reality, we're all lieutenants now."

"Lieutenants?" Hawk looked stunned. "We skip right over ensign?"

Fallon nodded. "Yeah. Apparently we'll need that rank to do things we need to do. But like I said, to everyone else, we're going to go right back to being regular cadets."

"Who cares?" Raptor said. "*We* know."

They laughed and joked until a knock on the door made them all turn.

Admiral Krazinski entered, looking distinguished and vaguely intimidating in his uniform with his rank insiginia on the shoulder. "Is it safe to enter? I tried to give you a little time to celebrate."

"Seems safe, sir," Peregrine said, in her deadpan style after bowing to him. "I'll vouch for your safety."

Krazinski grinned. "Well done, Avian Unit. Not too many teams think to bring the follow-drone. Very few jump out of the ship. For most, this is an unsolvable puzzle. Only a few have managed to line up the details enough to actually get here."

"Does that mean the others fail?" Peregrine asked.

"There's no pass or fail here," Krazinski said. "This is an exercise to teach you how much you don't know, and how desperately you're going to need skills. This exercise illustrates how deadly serious it is to be prepared for any number of situations, and to be able to critically think your way out of a tight spot." He paused, then continued, "Your second module will diverge from that of the other cadets. They'll all be doing official jobs on the campus and learning the ins and outs of daily officer life. You four will be cramming in as much survival training as possible. You'll learn to rappel and rock climb, survive in harsh conditions, and administer field medicine. I hope you're ready for this."

Fallon nodded.

"Definitely," Hawk said forcefully.

Krazinski smiled. "I believe that. I'm proud of you four. You're shaping up to be what I thought you could be. Keep working. I have to get going now, but my officers here know what to do. I'll be in touch."

Fallon wanted to stop him to ask questions. The past few days had made her feel a lot closer to her team, and the thought of going back to the OTS campus, where she still hadn't told them about Minho, made her uneasy. She didn't want to keep secrets anymore. But she wasn't sure if she should wait and let Minho reveal himself to the others at a time that would be most opportune for them. He had said that he'd be their mentor too.

But she could hardly say those things with the others right there. Instead, she bowed, thanked the admiral, and wished him safe travels.

She'd have to figure out the situation with Minho for herself.

WHILE THE FIRST module had been grindingly slow, the second one was anything but. Immediately, Fallon and her team began a schedule of trainings, simulations, and studies that required twelve-hour days, five days a week.

She rappelled, she climbed, she treated pretend flesh wounds, and she learned how to survive in a variety of harsh environments.

She'd never had so much fun or felt so tired.

Weekends were their time to rest, heal from sore muscles or minor injuries, and relax.

Most weekends, they met up at Lone Wolf Lowell's. Often, the four of them watched holo-vids together.

Hawk had even made some minor efforts to avoid eating all of everyone else's food. At least there was some effort involved.

Weeks went by and Fallon hadn't seen Minho. She wondered where he'd gone and what he was doing, but she stayed too busy to dwell on it.

Two months into the second module, she found herself with a night alone for a change. Hawk had a date, Raptor had gone to play cards with some friends he'd made during the first module, and Peregrine had simply said she'd be out.

Rather than cook, Fallon went to the mess hall. She ate slowly, then lingered, watching the other cadets. Her path had already diverged greatly from theirs, though they didn't know it.

She was already a lieutenant. And she'd been living under an assumed name for years.

She felt very different from the rest of them, as if they lived in a different reality. For all practical purposes, they did.

Only her team could really know or understand her.

She put away her dishes and tray and took the long way around campus to get back to her cabin.

It was a pleasant time of year. Autumn had arrived, bringing a change in the smell of the air and winds that rustled leaves. She'd always liked the autumn season. The well-landscaped campus looked particularly nice.

She sat on a bench to watch some cadets she didn't know playing discball. She wondered where she'd be, next autumn. Probably not on Earth. Maybe not on any planet. She could be assigned to any number of stations or outposts.

This might be the last Earth autumn she saw for a while.

She didn't feel sad about the possibility—merely curious to see what the future held.

She felt someone approach and sit on the other side of the bench. Great. She should have sat in the middle and put her legs sideways to discourage anyone from joining her and making small talk.

"Didn't know you were a discball fan," the newcomer said.

Fallon glanced over. Minho watched the casual game as if he were greatly interested.

"I'm not," she answered. "Just getting some fresh air."

"How've you been?" he asked. "I heard you did well on your survival test."

"Very well," she corrected.

He smiled.

"Where have you been?" Maybe she wasn't supposed to ask, but she asked anyway.

"Oh, you know. Assassinating world leaders and changing the course of history." He shrugged.

He could be lying, or he could be telling the truth. Either seemed equally likely.

"So what brings you back here?" she asked.

"You."

"Why?"

"An epic battle."

"Between me and you?" she asked.

"Definitely."

She brushed off the front of her shirt. "Okay, but you won't win."

"I will."

She squinted at him. "Worst retort ever. And no, you won't."

He grinned. "You pick the weapon."

"Oh, weapons this time? Hm. Knives and swords would be messy, so let's go with bo staff."

"One of my favorites," he said.

"Mine too. Should I go get my own?"

"No need. I have a spare you can borrow."

"How generous of you."

They smiled at each other. In unison, they stood and strode off in the direction of his place.

"Now that you're back, I'm going to tell my team about you," she announced.

"Are you?"

She wasn't going to doubt herself, regardless of what he said. "Yep. I don't want to keep anything from them."

"All right, then. Sounds like you've grown together."

She shrugged. She didn't want to talk about them to him. Or anyone. Avian Unit's secrets didn't belong anywhere outside of Avian Unit.

He smiled. "That's good."

When they got to the door, he gestured to it. "Would you care to do the honors? Since you did last time."

She rolled her eyes, and he whistled a little tune as he unlocked and opened the door.

They walked straight into his little dojo and he closed the door behind them.

"Need some water or something first?" he asked.

"Nope."

"Fine." He walked to the far side, selected two bo staffs, and walked back. He tossed her one. "Let's go."

He advanced before she even had a grip on her weapon. She got her hands on it, then bent at the waist and flipped it around her back and over her head, swinging the staff hard and fast before straightening.

He swiped at her leg, but she knocked his bo aside and struck at his head. He deflected.

Crack. Crack. Again and again they struck, parried, countered, and evaded.

Every time she thought she'd gotten her shot, he somehow got out of the way in time. She just couldn't hit him.

He couldn't hit her either, though.

Her forehead dripped sweat, making her hairline wet, and her shirt became damp and clingy. And on they went.

Time passed. They had to have been at it for over an hour. Fallon's shoulders started to ache. His strikes were so hard. She worried her fatigue would cause her to let one hit its target.

But he didn't seem as vigorous as he had been, either. He was sweating just as much.

"Should we call it another draw?" she asked, finding it hard to get the words out.

"Why?" he asked. "You afraid you're about to lose?"

"No. But I think we both see where this is going."

He stepped back, holding his bo straight out in front of him, then letting his arms fall. "Okay, then."

She let her arms drop too, and lightning-fast, he thwacked her across the chest.

"Never trust an opponent," he warned. "Even if it seems like they've given up. Sometimes, that's the moment that they're the most dangerous."

"Ow." She scowled at him. "I thought we were sparring, not imparting age-old wisdom."

"So you recognize my wisdom."

"Yeah. The crappy kind you get out of a cookie." She pointed her bo at him warningly.

He put his hands up. "I made my point. We're done."

She narrowed her eyes at him. Grinning, he tossed his bo away. "Satisfied?"

She whacked him across the chest, just as he'd done to her.

"Now I am." Picking up his staff, she put them both away properly in his weapons stand.

He had some nice weapons. She lingered to admire a naginata. "This is Japanese. My father had one of these."

"Do you know how to use it?" he asked.

"Of course. Though it doesn't have much practical application in modern battles."

He chuckled. "I suppose not. But you like weapons for their own sake, don't you? Just like I do."

She nodded slowly. "Do you like old action holo-vids? I've got a good one that has a really nice naginata battle."

"Are you asking me back to your place for a holo-vid?" He waggled his eyebrows at her suggestively.

"Yes. But not like that." She shook her head, smiling.

"Rats. I thought I'd punctured your armor. I guess I'm just not mighty enough."

"Hah. Do you want to watch the vid or not?"

He shrugged. "Sure. If you're not worried about your teammates seeing us."

"Nope. Today's the day you meet them, I think."

"All right. Can't say I haven't been curious about them. Mind if I change into something not sweaty and stinky?"

She waved toward his bedroom. "Please do."

When they got to her cabin, no one was there. Minho went in and made himself comfortable on the couch while she showered and changed into fresh clothing. When she emerged, smelling much better, he seemed right at home.

"So what's your vid protocol?" he asked. "Do I get snacks?"

She eyed him. "Do you need snacks?"

"If I say I do, then do I get snacks?"

She sighed. "What do you want?"

"Definitely something cold to drink. And I don't know. Something salty?"

"Snack mix and cold tea it is," she decided. "Unless Hawk ate it all."

She dumped some crackers, nuts, and pretzels into a bowl, mixed them up, and poured them each a tall glass of tea.

"Are you fancy?" she called. "Do you need a mint leaf?"

"Do you have a mint leaf?"

"No."

"Then why ask?"

She carried everything over on a tray. "Just being hospitable."

"Trying something new?" he teased.

She set his glass in front of him. "In case I ever need it as a cover identity."

"I see." He tossed some of the snack mix in his mouth and chewed. "Mm. Not bad. So what vid is this?"

She sat down and queued it up. "One of my favorites. A student's teacher goes missing, and he needs to use everything he's learned to rescue her from a crime syndicate."

The vid started, and Minho immediately exclaimed, "This is one of my favorites! Awesome."

They fell silent and settled in to happily watch.

When the teacher got poisoned, Minho threw a peanut at the vid. "What kind of coward uses poison? Boo!"

The nut sailed right through the projection and skittered across the floor.

Fallon stared at him. "I hope you're planning on picking that up."

He shrugged. "Later."

They went back to watching. When the hero got battered, they booed, and when he later got his redemption, they cheered.

"Take that, you honorless son of a grub!" Minho threw a cracker through the vid.

"Hey!" Fallon sat up straight. "Stop throwing food where I live!"

He made a face at her.

"Fine!" She reached into the bowl and threw a peanut at him, hitting him square in the chest.

He gaped at her. "Oh, no you didn't."

"Oh, yes I did."

His fingers twitched and moved toward the bowl.

"Don't. Even. Think about it," she hissed.

He made a grab, but she sprang across the couch and tackled him.

"Grappling! Great!" He twisted, preventing her from getting a lock on one of his joints, but she didn't give him any opportunities either.

"Rmph!" she complained when he mashed her face with his armpit. "Gross!"

They rolled and tumbled across the floor, each trying to get the advantage.

Then, to Fallon's horror, she heard the door open.

This surely didn't look good.

Sprawled across Minho, she turned to look over her shoulder.

Raptor stared at her in disbelief.

Well, shit.

Then she saw Peregrine and Hawk behind him.

Triple shit.

Peregrine and Hawk, in all their wisdom, immediately took off toward their rooms.

"Night!" Hawk called.

"Wait!" Fallon flipped over and got to her feet. She straightened her shirt. "It's not what you think."

Hawk slowly turned around. "If that's true, then I'm both relieved and disappointed, and I'm not sure which I feel more deeply. But please do explain this. I'm listening."

Peregrine faced them, but she continued edging backward, stealing glances at Raptor.

"This isn't how I saw this going," Fallon muttered, then cleared her throat. "Okay. Guys, this is Minho. He's been assigned as a mentor for us."

"Exactly what is he mentoring you in?" Hawk raised an eyebrow at Minho, who sat on the floor, looking extremely disheveled.

"We were actually grappling just now because he threw a nut..." she sighed. "Yeah, that didn't sound right. I mean, we were sparring. Nothing weird."

Hawk puckered his lips. "Sadly, I believe you. Okay, Mentor Minho, let's hear your introduction."

Minho looked to Fallon, but she shrugged. He was on his own.

He stood and gave them the shallow bow of an equal. It was a kindness to do so, since he outranked them. "This isn't how I pictured meeting you, but hello. I'm Minho. I'm a mechanical specialist. And...I'm not sure what else to say."

Raptor, usually the one to smooth everything over and make everyone feel instantly at ease, stood silently, looking from Fallon to Minho.

Peregrine stepped forward and bowed, the gesture of a subordinate to a superior. "I'm Peregrine of Avian Unit. Small electronics and master of disguise."

She said it without smiling, which made Minho grin.

Hawk made a proper but quick bow. "Hawk. I get shit done. Yadda yadda."

Fallon detected a glint of humor in Minho's eyes.

Raptor's voice was reserved when he said, "Raptor. Hacking and infiltration."

He didn't bow.

"I'm glad to meet you all. I won't be around all the time, but when I am, you can talk to me about any of your concerns. I won't be able to answer all your questions, but I'll try to keep you on the right track and help with what I can. Sometimes just having someone who's been through it can be a big help."

"Great," Hawk said. "Looking forward to that. For now, though, I'm going to excuse myself from this very uncomfortable situation." He bowed, more politely this time, and left.

"I kind of think he has the right idea." Peregrine bowed and went to her room.

"I'm sure you'll be helpful." Raptor bowed and turned sharply, retreating to his own room.

Fallon sighed. "Well, you sure screwed that up."

"Me?" Minho blinked at her. "You were the one who jumped on me."

"Don't say that so loudly," she hissed. "They already have the wrong idea."

"So you and Raptor..." Minho trailed off.

"Yeah. We were. I mean, we're working on it. We ended things after the academy, for the good of the team."

"Did you?" Minho looked doubtful.

"Well...mostly." She cringed. "Like I said, we're working on it."

"I see. Well, good luck with that. I'll be on my way to let you deal with it." He walked across the room and picked up the nut and the cracker he'd tossed. "Thank you for a lovely evening." He bowed, then ducked out the door before she should return the bow.

Alone, she sighed.

She straightened the couch, turned off the holo-vid, and cleaned up the snack mix. Then she took care of the snack bowl and the glasses. When she could put it off no longer, she went to Raptor's room and knocked on the door.

Rap rap rap. Three times. Confidently, but not aggressively.

After a long pause that had her thinking about knocking again, the door opened. Raptor stepped back to let her in, saying nothing.

A silent Raptor was a very bad, very disturbing thing.

"There's nothing going on with Minho and me," she said.

"How long have you been seeing him?"

"I'm not *seeing* him as in dating him," she stressed. "But I met him a little while after OTS started. His primary focus at that time was helping me figure out how to be the leader of Avian Unit."

"Did he order you to keep that from us?" Raptor asked.

"No. I made that decision. As the leader, I felt it was important to keep our focus on one another, and not bring another person into the mix yet."

"Why didn't you tell me that?"

Her guts shifted uncomfortably. "This is what we were worried about. That our being together would create a special loyalty between us that isolated Hawk and Peregrine. Remember?"

He looked past her, at the wall. "Yeah. Yeah. I know." He let out a long sigh. "Of course that's why. And I figured we'd both eventually date other people. I get what you'd see in him, but I just didn't expect you to move on so soon."

"I haven't."

"You were on top of him."

"We really were just grappling. It was just kind of...playful. He and I have the same fighting style and we like challenging each other. It's competitive and fun. But that's it." She reached out and took his hands, forcing him to look at her. "How could I have moved on? If it were going to be anyone, it would be you. I've tried, but I can't get over you."

He curled his fingers around hers. "I'm not over you, either."

"There have been times," she admitted, "that I have to remind myself not to lean against you or reach for your hand."

"Yeah. Same here."

"How many times has it happened to you?"

He shrugged. "Oh, I don't know, just all the time."

He smiled, and she smiled back. They stood facing each other, smiling like fools.

The world shrank down around them, and she felt like he was all that existed. At the very least, he was all that mattered, in that moment.

It had always been like this with him. This feeling of belonging.

She should step back. She should pull her hands free of his. They'd made a pragmatic choice for a logical reason when they'd agreed they couldn't be together. They should stick to it.

But she didn't step back and didn't pull her hands free.

Instead, she leaned into him. Leaned into his warmth, his laughter, and the understanding she'd never find anywhere else.

7

FALLON EXPECTED to get some extreme teasing from Hawk the next morning. She escaped from Raptor's room through the connecting bathroom and emerged a carefully timed twelve minutes after he went to the kitchen.

"Did you eat all the bread again?" Peregrine asked, looking into an empty bread container. "Seriously. How am I supposed to make toast?"

Looking guilty, Hawk held out a piece of toast toward her. "Sorry. I wake up really hungry."

She took the toast. "You're in charge of bringing in some groceries today."

She pointed the toast at him, giving him a severe look, then took a bite.

Fallon approached cautiously, making sure she kept distance between her and Raptor. She avoided looking at him too much, but didn't avoid looking in his direction altogether, because that would have been too obvious.

This was maddening. Had it been worth it?

She turned to peer into the cooler and smiled where no one else could see. Yeah, it had been worth it.

Officially, she didn't have a past. So far, she didn't have any concrete picture of her future. All she could do was live for right now and make decisions as they came at her.

One thing at a time.

Rather than a full breakfast, she got herself a protein bar and some juice.

"Is that all you're having?" Hawk asked, looking at the items in her hands like they were toxic.

"Just for now. I haven't gone for a run yet." She leaned against the counter, rather than sitting down, and opened the protein bar. "I'll eat some more after. Running on a full stomach makes me nauseated. Anyone want to run with me?"

She hadn't yet had much luck in getting the others to do a morning run. Hawk and Peregrine were far from morning people, and, of course, she and Raptor had been careful not to spend much time alone.

But Raptor said, "Sure. We don't have our new schedules yet, so I'm just wandering around. Might as well get in some cardio."

Just when Fallon thought no one was going to mention Minho, Hawk straightened as if he'd just woken up.

"So, that Minho guy," he said. "What's his deal?"

"I'm not sure he has a deal," Fallon answered. "He's supposed to help us. He's already done what we're doing now." She shrugged. "That makes him the voice of experience. We could use that."

"Has he told you anything useful? Like what comes next?" Peregrine asked, finishing her last bite of toast.

"It's not like that. He doesn't just lay out a bunch of information. When I saw Krazinski, he didn't tell me much, either. It seems like they want us to get used to living in a need-to-know kind of limbo. If we don't need to know it right then, they won't tell us, so we either don't know or we have to figure it out ourselves."

Hawk scratched at his stubble. "You think that's, like, conditioning us to get used to living in the dark and just doing what we're told without knowing why?"

"Probably."

He went on as if she hadn't spoken. "Or maybe they want to push us to be more proactive. To find things out on our own."

Peregrine chewed on the pad of her thumb. "Possible."

"I think you'll like Minho, though," Fallon said. "I wasn't sure I did, at first, but then I got to understand him a little better."

"Is he a team leader?" Raptor asked.

"Yeah. That's why he focused on me first."

"Where's the rest of his team, then?" Hawk asked.

"Dead," Fallon said quietly. "I'm not sure what happened, but he's the only one left."

"So," Hawk said, "is he supposed to teach you what not to do? Because I'm kind of aiming higher, at not dying."

It was a rude, inappropriate thing to say, but Fallon smiled faintly. "We can hope. I mean, it would be a shame if I had to cause your grisly demise just to save my own skin."

"Hah." Hawk grinned and went back to eating.

"I'd do it, though," she assured him. "Just so you know."

He knew she wouldn't. And she knew he knew it too.

"Are you ready?" she asked Raptor, when he seemed to be done eating. "I'm ready to run."

"Yeah, just let me change. You go ahead and get a head start. I'll catch up."

"You wish." She laughed at him as he retreated to his room.

She waited by the door. Module two, thus far, had turned out to be infinitely better than module one. She hoped module three would prove to be the best of all.

"PRELIN'S ASS," Hawk swore. "He's bleeding everywhere. I can't stop it." His hands pressed down on a very bloody chest in a vain attempt to stop the flow.

"Pressure isn't enough," Raptor said. "Hang on. I need to seal off an artery." He muttered under his breath, trying to find the right angle to get to the artery.

"There. There. Now quick, inject him with some synthblood before his pressure drops too much."

Fallon used a hypo to find a good vein and begin the synthblood transfusion.

"Hang on, pressure's dropping too much. Peregrine, give him a pace or he's going to go into arrest."

Peregrine pressed a device to the patient's shoulder to keep the cardiac muscle beating.

"Good. Good." Raptor muttered under his breath some more as he sealed the wound. Once he had it successfully healed, he said much more energetically, "Good! He's going to make it!"

All four of them cheered. It was their first non-fatal application of field medicine.

They completed the job, sealing the wound, cleaning the patient, and putting dermacare bandages over the brand-new skin.

In the end, they were covered in blood, but jubilant.

"Good." Dr. Delco stepped in, examining their work. "Not perfect, but good. You can shut it off now."

Hawk hit the switch and the synthetic simulacrum went still.

Raptor, as it turned out, had a knack for field medicine. Soon after they'd begun, it had been assigned to him as his secondary specialty.

The others all had to learn too, of course. They'd each have to save a patient on their own before they could pass this part of the module. But for today, "saving" this simulacrum from pretend death was a victory.

"Go get cleaned up," Dr. Delco ordered. "Tomorrow, we'll start on head wounds."

"I wish that meant giving them, not treating them." Hawk spoke in a low voice so the doctor wouldn't hear.

Fallon stifled her laughter until they got out of the medbay.

THE SECOND MODULE flew by in a rush of simulated blood and wounds, dire survival situations, and a growing feeling that Fallon had never experienced before. The more she and her team worked together, the more connected to them she felt. The more they felt like an extension of herself. When she helped Hawk build a fire, she knew exactly how to hand the wood off to him. When she was assisting Raptor with a patient, she could anticipate his orders.

Peregrine was the quietest of them, and though she didn't make a lot of noise, Fallon could more easily read her microexpressions and body language. Peregrine had opinions, all right. Lots of them. She just didn't air them unless she decided it served a purpose.

She was a solid, steady weight that never complained and always supported. The more they worked together, the more Fallon realized how critical that was. Before, she never would have thought that would matter at all.

Minho hadn't dropped by since his initial introduction to the team, which was a little odd, but Fallon stayed too busy to notice. She had little energy to give to anything outside of her team.

Raptor, though, did receive a bit more of her energy than her other two teammates did. They'd moved on to a different version of their relationship.

They had never, even back at the academy, used words like boyfriend or girlfriend for one another, or exchanged I-love-yous. They didn't do that now, either, and they'd adopted a low-key approach to being together.

Often, one of them went through the connecting bathroom to

the other's room, but they were as likely to stay up talking into the night as anything else. Though the "anything else" happened on occasion, too. They decided that as long as they kept it casual and didn't consider themselves a couple, this level of intimacy couldn't hurt the team. Raptor had assured her that he wouldn't expect her to be any more forthcoming with him about team affairs, or treat him differently than Peregrine or Hawk when it came to anything relating to Avian Unit.

Their relationship could simply be low-key, and entirely unrelated to the team. Why keep making things awkward by trying to repress their feelings, anyway? It seemed to create more issues that it solved.

Together, the four of them forged forward, learning and growing into what they needed to be. After two days of desert survival training, Fallon found herself exhausted but surprisingly happy with the direction things were going.

On the way back to the cabin, Hawk had pretty much threatened Peregrine's life over getting the first shower, and heavily implied that Fallon and Raptor's shower wasn't safe, either, and that they should watch their dusty, dirty backs.

She ignored his over-the-top threats of violence and gave Raptor the first shower in their shared bathroom.

"You sure?" he asked.

"Yeah. Please. Go first. You stink like I can't even tell you." She put a hand over her nose.

"Hate to tell you, partner," he said, looking cute even with his face grimy and smelling like a garbage truck, "but you don't smell like flowers and sunshine, either."

"Hurry, or I'll change my mind," she warned.

He disappeared into the bathroom.

She hoped he'd be quick. She was so sandy and gritty that she didn't dare sit on her bed or anywhere else. She'd left her shoes and her jacket outside to deal with later.

She leaned against the doorframe, imagining a cool, crystal clear pool. Ahh. The smell of hyacinths and jasmine and...

The door opened. "Your turn."

Raptor wore a towel around his waist and a smile. Then he grimaced and put a hand over his nose. "Damn, you smell even worse now."

She made claw-hands at him with her dusty, dirty hands. He made an "eep!" sound and ran into his room.

Laughing, she got into the shower and turned on the water.

Ahhhhh. There was nothing like a hydro shower. Sonic showers just didn't provide the same feeling of getting clean. As she stood under the water, letting steam curl up toward the air evac intakes, she hoped she wouldn't get assigned to a ship or a station that didn't have hydro showers, for at least a few years.

She could take a lot of deprivation, punishment, and pain, but a good, steamy hydro shower was the one solace she didn't think she could do without in the long term.

As she tried to get the sand out of her hair, she envied Raptor's short hairstyle. Hers was only just past shoulder length, and she wore it in a ponytail most of the time. But even at that length, she was pretty sure she'd brought back a desert's worth of sand. It seemed to take forever to get it out. Every time she thought she'd gotten it squeaky clean, she found more grit.

Maybe she should think about a shorter style.

Finally, she felt clean enough to shut off the water, wrap herself in a towel, and trudge back to her room.

The last thing she wanted to see was Minho, standing by the window.

She borrowed one of Hawk's favorite swears. "Oh, Prelin's ass!"

FALLON REFUSED to be embarrassed by wearing a towel, having

her hair dripping down her back, and her shoulders bare and damp.

She had a toned, muscular body, and she was proud of it. Let Minho be uncomfortable if he had a problem with what she was wearing—or wasn't. He was the one who had barged into her room uninvited.

Again.

She had a sudden moment of feeling at one with Hawk. She was pretty sure he'd have approached the situation the same way.

No, entirely sure.

"What?" she snapped. "I am entirely too tired for any shit today."

"The work we do doesn't care about being tired. You do what you need to do, when you need to do it, and that's all there is to it. Put on your uniform."

"No."

Minho blinked. "What was that, cadet?"

"I said no. Whatever exercise you have planned right now, forget it. I won't allow my team to be involved. Right now, each one of them is exhausted. If you push them, for the sake of teaching them some lesson, they'll be injured. More importantly, if we're in a dangerous situation, something serious could happen. Shit happens when shit happens. I get that. We'll deal with that when a real situation arises. You can write me up for a reprimand if you want, but right now, I'm not going to let you abuse my team just for training purposes."

When she stopped speaking, she realized she'd advanced on him several steps, and was now standing so close that she could see the tiny freckle by his left eye.

"All right, then," Minho said.

"What?"

"All right. The others can stay here. I'll take you by yourself."

She hesitated. She was exhausted. But if it meant that the

others could get some sleep, she'd do it. She struggled to find some energy from deep within. "Fine."

"Fail." Minho shook his head. "And you were doing so well, too."

"What?" She felt like she kept saying that.

"You stood up for your team. Protected them. That was good. But then you sacrificed yourself. What good do you think you are as a leader if you aren't in good enough shape to lead? This is always the problem with leaders. They're too willing to self sacrifice. But you can't. The strongest thing you can do is protect yourself, so that you can protect your team. Understand?"

"But how do I protect them and myself at the same time?" It seemed like an impossible situation. "Sometimes one thing has to be sacrificed, to save the other."

"You'll find that with experience. But first, you have to get the hero complex out of your head. You're not here to take a bullet for your team. You might do that, at some point, but only if it's the right choice. Or simply unavoidable. You're not their shield. You're their leader. There might come a point where one of you has to be sacrificed for the others. Maybe that one should be you, but more likely, it's one of them. There is no glory in death. There's only death in death. You have to give up your hero complex and make the right choice for the team."

"How could I ever choose one of them over me?" She couldn't imagine ever choosing to send Hawk, Peregrine, or Raptor to their death if she could prevent it.

"If you can't, you don't deserve to be their leader. They depend on you to give the right order. Maybe your death would be the right choice. But maybe it would only assure that others would go with you. You have to be able to make the right choice for the situation. And you can't hesitate when you do it."

She tried to imagine it. Sending Hawk to his death, to save Peregrine and Raptor. She whispered, "I don't know if I could do that. They're my team."

Minho nodded. "I know. But you've got to start thinking about that now, before you're in those life and death situations. You've got to train your mind to filter out your feelings and make the best strategic course, both for the members of your team and for the mission."

She leaned against the wall. "I can't let them die."

He put his hand on her bicep. "You might have to. I think it's time I told you about my team."

AFTER FALLON PUT on some lounge clothes and towel dried her hair, she called her team out to the living area. Minho wanted to tell her about his team, but she wanted them to hear too. Whatever it was, it had to be bad, and she didn't want to keep it from them.

Hawk looked particularly bent about having to engage with others, and made a point of lounging on the couch with his legs open, wearing no shirt.

Fallon felt pretty certain he shot Minho some come-hither glances too. She wasn't sure whether Hawk had an actual interest in Minho, or if he just wanted to harass him.

Minho sat cross-legged on the floor, almost as if about to meditate. He certainly didn't seem concerned about Hawk's attention.

So that they weren't all looking downward at Minho, Fallon sat on the floor too.

It was natural for her, since she often sat on the floor in front of the couch, anyway. She'd always had a habit of leaning back against furniture rather than sitting on it.

She did that now, focusing her complete attention on Minho.

He let out a breath. "This isn't a story I like to retell, and once I do it, I'm never going to talk about it to you again."

He closed his eyes. "I had a four-person team. They're not all four. Some have five. Some have had six. It's all about the mix of skills and personalities, and abilities to get certain kinds of jobs done."

Fallon wanted to ask what kinds of jobs, but kept her mouth shut. If she cut Minho off, she sensed that he might stop talking altogether.

He continued, "We had two men, a woman, and a Kanaran. I'd never met a Kanaran, and just adjusting to the pronouns was hard." He smiled at the memory. "But my partner was forgiving and didn't take offense. They should have, probably, but they didn't. My Kanaran partner had a certain kindness that I've never seen in anyone else. And the other guy was unique in his own way."

He paused. "I'm not going to tell you names, or what planets they were from. That's not because I don't think you're trustworthy. It's because I'm protecting their identities. Understand?"

When they all nodded, Minho mused, "Even after they've all been dead for over a year, I still protect them. Or, more precisely, their families." He looked down at his hands. "We do things, you see, in black ops, that could hurt the people we've left behind. Families, friends, whoever we knew in our past lives. Even after we die, knowledge of us can hurt them. It's a deep rabbit hole we go down, and you can never come out again. It's not just any black ops. Even the PAC's official intelligence department has a clandestine division. But those people can get back out. Those of us who go into Blackout don't."

He fell silent for a few beats. "Hang with me here. This isn't a story I tell, so I'm working at it as I go. I might need some time here and there to figure out how I want to say it."

Fallon and her team remained silent.

Minho continued, "I think it's fair to say that we weren't significantly different from you four. Our details were different. Our team name was different. Our skills were different. But in the ways that mattered, we were much the same. We learned each other over time—we grew together, we fought together, and we trusted each other. There's a reason I waited this long to tell you this story. Why do you think that is?"

Fallon waited, but when none of her teammates spoke up, she did. "Because we weren't close enough yet."

Minho nodded. "Exactly. You still aren't there, but the framework is in place. It will keep tightening as you go. But you can now understand what I'm talking about. A few months ago, you wouldn't have."

Minho heaved a sigh and smiled ruefully. "I feel like I need a drink. But I want to say this as clearly as possible. Okay. So my team and I were tight. Like you're getting to be, but moreso, because we'd been on several missions together.

We finished up one mission, had some leave time, then went to Jamestown for new orders. That's how it tends to go. One mission after another, with some downtime between. You don't always get the downtime, but the admirals do try to see that we get it whenever possible. They know we need time to process, recover, and reset. Anyway, the new orders weren't like our other missions. This one was a deep infiltration. Long term. We were expected to be on this for up to three years."

Minho fell silent, apparently lost in thought. Maybe he was replaying memories in his head, remembering how things had happened. He didn't look sad, merely nostalgic and thoughtful.

"We got deep into a non-PAC planet's infrastructure. We did some things we wouldn't have in any other situation. Things that are bad. But they were necessary so that we could get ahead of some other things, things that threatened the PAC itself. So bad things, but smaller bad things, so that we could do bigger good things."

He ran a hand through his hair. "I know that sounds stupid. Juvenile. But it's what it breaks down to. We committed some relatively minor offenses in the effort of preventing major offenses. We didn't love that, but only a terrible person would like it. So we did what we had to do, and when the moment came, we struck."

He clasped his hands together. "It went wrong. We had bad intel. The person we thought was on our side was most definitely not on our side. We ended up in a situation where one of us had to stay behind to save the others."

His expression tightened. "I stayed behind. I wanted them to get away, to get the job done, protect the PAC, and go on living. But since they didn't have their mechanics specialist, they got stuck. They fought hard, but they all died. And in the end, I made it out only because that government wanted to use me as a political pawn against the PAC. It was everything that could go wrong in a mission."

He blew out a breath and opened his hands wide. "So here I am. Alive, while my team is long dead. I'll never have another team. I'm twenty-four years old and a lone operator in Blackout. Do you know how useless that is? And how much I hate every day, knowing that my team died because I couldn't sacrifice one of them for the other two?"

He let those words hang in the air. After a long minute, Minho spoke again. "I'm here to see that what happened to my team doesn't happen to yours. I'm a living cautionary tale. My penance for their deaths is preventing yours."

Fallon tried to imagine it. Twenty-four years old, and it was already over for him. His team was gone, and he was left to keep going forward.

"What was your team name?" she asked. "Surely it can't hurt to know that."

For a moment, she thought he wouldn't answer. Then he said, "Flame. We were Flame unit."

The room fell silent. It was hard to know what to say in the face of such a tragic story that, for all Fallon knew, could happen to them, too.

It could happen to any team. Blackout existed because clandestine things had to be done for the good of the PAC, and because someone had to take those risks.

"I'm sorry you lost them," Peregrine said. "It wasn't your fault."

"It was." Minho said it matter-of-factly. "Not maliciously, but if I'd left one of the others to die, I could have gotten the other two out of there. Just because I was trying to sacrifice myself for them doesn't mean I'm not responsible for their deaths."

Fallon wanted to offer comforting words, but he was right. He'd made the wrong call. His people had died. He now had to live with that.

She tried to imagine giving up Hawk so Peregrine and Raptor could live. Or any other combination.

She couldn't imagine it. But at least she now had Minho, in the back of her mind, telling her to make the brutal choice, for the good of the rest.

She looked down at the floor. It was a lot to think about.

"Now that I've entirely ruined your post-mission buzz," Minho said, "I'll let myself out."

"Wait," Raptor said. "Hang on. If you don't have a team, and you're here to help us..." he looked to Fallon. "And she thinks you're not a total shitweasel...then why don't you become our unofficial fifth member?"

Fallon wasn't sure what to react to first—the use of the word "shitweasel" or the honorary membership.

In either case, Minho smiled. "That's a kind offer. If you still feel that way after OTS—and if you're not worried I'm going to steal your woman—I'll accept."

"What woman?" Raptor asked. "I have no woman!"

Fallon added, "I'm not anybody's woman."

Hawk scooted closer to Fallon and put a big, heavy arm around her. "I keep trying to make her my woman, but she keeps turning me down."

Peregrine smirked.

Fallon slapped Hawk's arm.

"Ow," he complained, grinning. "I think a gnat bit me."

Minho smiled faintly, which, considering the mood just a moment ago, seemed like a victory. "Thanks, guys. You should get some rest, though. I'll see you tomorrow afternoon."

Peregrine stared at him. "Wait. Why?"

Minho grinned. "Zero-g maneuvers. I don't recommend a big breakfast."

AS MUCH AS Minho seemed to be on their side, he pushed them hard.

First, there was the barfing in zero-g. As a team, they agreed that they'd never reveal who had lost it and who hadn't. But it hadn't been pretty.

Then, they'd gone on to deprivation. Pain tolerance. Starvation tolerance.

That last one, of course, was hardest on Hawk, and no one could deny it.

Module two hurt. But there were worse things than hurting.

For the first time, Fallon truly felt like Fallon—not Emiko or Kiyoko or any other name she'd ever been known by. She wasn't pretending to be Fallon. She'd *become* Fallon. She earned that name with blood, sweat, and tears—literally.

Then they made it through to the other side. When they reached the end of the second module, it came as a surprise. Fallon had just gotten her stride.

Hawk, Peregrine, and Raptor felt the same.

"You've earned a vacation," Krazinski said. "Take two weeks off and go anywhere on the planet, expenses paid. You've earned it."

"No."

The four members of Avian Unit had found their stride. They didn't need, or want, a vacation.

"Bring it on," they said. "We're ready."

And so their own, personal module three began.

"OH, PRELIN'S ASS, YEAH." Hawk had never looked so happy.

He stood in a weapons locker, wearing a belt of ammo, holding what amounted to a cannon and looking like he'd just found his reason for existence.

Fallon could relate.

If this was module three, she couldn't even fathom module four. She stood, surrounded by weapons, ammunition, body shields, and armor.

If she'd known there was a place like this, she would have made sure to get here a whole lot sooner.

Even Peregrine wore a cool, serene smile. Or maybe it was a smirk. It looked queenly, whatever it was, as she stood there with an RPG on her shoulder.

"Yeah," she sighed. "That's nice."

Raptor was the only one who didn't seem quite as enraptured as the others. "So...nothing of this is connected to a larger network? I can't hack into any of this? What's the point?"

Fallon stood, holding a pair of rifles that immediately made her arms tired. She didn't let on, though. "The point is...*bang bang bang*, flame, fire, mayhem, let's get outta here!"

She imagined a whole scenario in a scant five seconds.

"Yeah!" Hawk agreed.

It wasn't an articulated, well-reasoned response, but his enthusiasm made up for it, in her opinion.

"I'm not sure I'm going to love this module," Raptor mused as Fallon poked through the weapons inventory.

Either you liked firepower or you didn't. It seemed that Raptor wasn't that type.

After a moment's thought, Fallon decided that she liked him anyway.

She put on a weapons belt and challenged herself to see how many items she could stash in it. Three stingers, five knives, and two pseudo-rifles seemed to be the limit.

More than that, and the sheer weight of it would probably drag it down to her knees.

"So this is what it's like," Peregrine said, looking deeply thoughtful.

Fallon looked up from all the power and energy around her to study her partner. "What do you mean?"

Peregrine looked at her. "When the other girls were having tea parties, serving each other pretend tea made of air, and eating air cookies, and wearing pretend jewels and tiaras. This is what they were pretending."

Fallon was pretty sure those little girls hadn't been pretending to wear a bandolier full of high-caliber ammo, as Peregrine was. But she had to admit that Peregrine looked like a goddess of war.

"Yep," she agreed. "Totally the same thing."

Peregrine smiled. A real, genuine smile. With teeth and everything.

Fallon almost took a step back from the sheer shock.

Oh, hell yeah, the third module of OTS was going to be amazing. No doubt about it.

8

SHE WAS WRONG. Fallon had misjudged. Module three sucked. At least, at that moment, it did. She lay on the ground, wearing full body armor, unable to breathe from the bullet that had just struck her full force in the chest.

A genuine, real, live round. Right in her chest. Armor or not, it hurt like hell. Pain became an ocean that lived in her chest, flowing and rolling and weighing her lungs down.

"Sucks, right?" Minho squatted down next to her head. "Remember how that feels. Lethal blow or not, it can still incapacitate you. Which can mean you die, all the same. Don't get hit."

She had no breath to answer.

Instead, she mentally ran through all of Hawk's favorite swear words. There was something about them. Chanting them, even silently in her mind, was like an incantation that helped ward off some of the burning, black ache that seemed to make a wasteland of her chest area.

Prelin's ass, it hurt like nothing she'd ever felt.

Tears streamed out of the corners of her eyes and she wasn't even crying.

Hands lifted her, stripped her armor, and moved her. Hands she trusted.

Her team.

The others would do this too. They'd take the hit, just to learn how it felt. And she'd lift them, too. She'd peel off their armor, and tend to their hurts.

They were hers, and she was theirs.

They were a team.

She closed her eyes, and entrusted herself to them.

SHE NEARLY DROWNED. She nearly suffocated. She shot, fought, and struggled her way forward.

Module three was pain. Module three was torture. Module three left Fallon with barely enough will to wake up the next day.

But most days, she woke up beside Raptor. Her first thoughts went to Hawk and Peregrine, no matter how much her body ached.

And just like that, she got up again. She'd see them through the day, whatever it took.

Her relationship with Raptor had changed again, at least for the time being. The other things were still beneath the surface, but there was nothing romantic or sexy about dragging each other to a flat surface, applying dermacare patches, and falling into an abyss of sleep.

Sometimes she woke up near Hawk, too. Sleep location no longer mattered. The peace of unconsciousness and the promise of healing, however, did.

She began to hate Minho. Not as a person, but as a harbinger. Whenever he showed up, she knew bad shit was going to go down.

But on they went, week after week. Weapons. Survival. Pain.

"Why?" she'd cried once, no longer embarrassed by crying. Her arm, leg, and multiple ribs had been broken. Her body was a deep abyss of agony that made her blind to anything her eyes could see.

Everyone cried, once they'd been broken down hard enough. Minho had held her and tucked her hair behind her ear. "To help you live," he said.

Sleeping. Waking. Weapons. Fighting. Pain. Waiting.

Fallon hated Module three. Hated it like she'd never hated anything.

Then she got through it.

She healed, she persevered, and she made it to the other side.

She was the same person, but she felt different.

"What now?" Hawk asked one morning in their cabin. "We have two weeks before the last module. We're all healed and we have no assignments. What do we do?"

She liked that he assumed they'd spend those two weeks together. Even Peregrine didn't drift away to get distance. She stayed right there with them, quiet but loudly present, in her own way.

"What do you want to do?" Fallon asked.

Hawk lifted his chin, looking downright philosophical. "I'm thinking waterpark."

Fallon laughed.

"I'm serious," Hawk said. "Let's go somewhere that no one is shooting at us or trying to kick our asses. Let's go somewhere that it's all fun and games. I'll win you some big, stuffed, ugly thing," he promised.

So they went. They went on water rides that drenched them, thrill rides that were fun without the real threat of danger—unless you counted a mechanical failure and subsequent death, which Fallon no longer did—and extremely unhealthy snacks.

She'd changed, though. Even as she ate fried foods and

laughed with her team, she had an eye out. Watching for anything unusual. Keeping them from having their backs to a doorway. Always calculating a way out from whatever scenario she was in.

She'd changed. And so had they.

And that was the point.

When the final module of OTS started, Fallon felt fifty years older than when she'd started.

Minho's next announcement didn't change that feeling.

He arrived at the cabin one evening as Fallon and the others were making dinner together, joking, laughing, and throwing a significant number of insults at one another.

Hawk answered the door, and when Minho stepped in, they all paused.

"Wow, I guess that tells me how much you guys still like me," Minho joked.

"We're just used to you being the one to bring news of painful things," Fallon said. She, for one, felt no differently about Minho just because he'd been forced to become the messenger. She appreciated his tireless hours of effort in training them.

She was pretty sure the others felt the same way, even though his arrival suggested potentially upsetting news.

"Depends on how you look at it," Minho said. "This is your last week residing at OTS. Your final module will be off-planet."

He looked from one face to the next, judging the reaction.

Fallon shrugged.

Peregrine went back to measuring rice to put into the heat-ex.

Raptor and Hawk looked likewise unmoved.

"Should I ask where we're going?" Hawk asked. "Or should I just assume it's classified?"

Minho made a self-deprecating gesture. "I know, I've been the bringer of bad news lately. But I think you'll like this one."

"Oh?" Raptor turned and gave him his full attention, as did the rest of them.

Some good news would be a welcome change.

Minho looked to Fallon. "You fly, right?"

"I do," she agreed.

He looked to Hawk. "And you shoot, right?"

"Damn right," Hawk affirmed with gusto.

Minho smiled. "Then yeah. You're definitely going to like this. Be packed up and ready to go in three days, because things are about to change."

FALLON RODE the orbital elevator up to the docking station above Earth. She'd done it before and the long wait and long ride were nothing special.

She walked across the station with Minho, which, other than the company of him and her team, was also not at all special.

But then they arrived at the docking slip where her assigned ship waited for her.

And, Prelin's ass, that was something special, indeed.

"Wow," she breathed, looking at the ship.

It was new, with no little pock marks or oxidizing discolorations on it. It had a state of the art propulsion chamber, a sleek design, and twinkled just the slightest bit because of its running lights.

It was beautiful.

Hawk put a heavy hand on her shoulder. "If you keep standing there, we can't actually board it."

"Ten more seconds," she pleaded, admiring the beauty of such a ship. She let out a breath. "Okay. Let's go."

After making sure the bags they hadn't carried had arrived ahead of them, thanks to the transit hub's delightfully efficient system, Fallon made a straight line toward the ship's bridge.

It was either new or had just been treated to a complete overhaul. Everything was pristine.

She paused, taking a deep breath of new-ship smell.

Minho had come up to the bridge with her. The others had preferred to check out their quarters first.

"What are you doing?" Minho asked.

"Smelling it."

He did a few test sniffs. "Are you messing with me?"

"No. Don't you smell it?"

He took a step back. "Yeah, you're definitely messing with me."

She chuckled. "No, a new ship has a different smell than others. I don't know what it is. Maybe it's leftover adhesive or something. Or maybe it's just how a ship smells before people muck it up with our skin oils and exhalations and dead skin cells."

"Ew." Minho grimaced. "When you put it that way, space travel sounds kind of disgusting."

"Oh, those things are everywhere people are. That's not something special about ships, other than their having a containment system."

"That doesn't make me feel better," he said.

She smiled. "Have you been on this ship before?"

"Nope. I'm seeing it for the first time too."

She pressed, "Do I get to know our destination now? I mean, we're going to have to put in some coordinates."

"Should I tell you ahead of the rest of the team?"

She shook her head. "Nope. We should hear it together. But we can gather everyone if you're ready to tell us."

"Let's let everyone settle in, then we'll call a meeting."

She liked the sound of that.

"IT's time for you four to see Jamestown." Minho sat in the mess hall, sitting at a round table along with Fallon and her team.

She fought down the urge to cheer. She hadn't even dared to hope that she'd finally get a look at PAC command. The timing didn't seem to work, though.

"Uh...it takes four months to get to Jamestown from Earth," she said.

Minho smiled. "In most ships, yes. This isn't most ships. I assume you noticed that it doesn't coincide with any other model of ship you've ever seen."

"I did, yes," she agreed.

"What else did you notice about this ship?" he asked.

"No weapons. Thick exterior plating. A huge propulsion chamber. My guess is that there's no cargo bay."

"Nicely done. Yes. This ship is little more than a rocket. It's made to withstand unusual stresses, has less mass and more shielding than standard ships, and after a flight, requires a full strip and rebuild because it burns out almost all its systems. Once they cool down upon arrival, the ship bricks itself."

"I've never heard of a ship like that," Fallon said.

"Blackout has toys that no one else does. Keep in mind that this is highly classified information, and if you breathe even a suggestion of this ship to anyone not inside Blackout, your career, and your life as you know it are over." Minho arched an eyebrow and smiled.

She exchanged a look with her teammates. Though the words were threatening, they didn't mind. The idea of actually getting on the inside of even just one of Blackout's secrets was thrilling.

"So how long will it take us to get there?" Fallon asked.

"Two months. In the meantime, I'll be teaching you about Jamestown, covert mission protocols, and some other classified technology that only we know about."

Fallon loved the sound of that. Finally, she felt like a member of Blackout. The inner circle.

"Even so," she said, "we'll barely have time to get to

Jamestown and back for graduation. Unless...we're not attending graduation?"

She wouldn't mind. She didn't need a ceremony to tell her she'd made it through OTS. She had already become an officer.

"Oh, you'll be there. It's part of your cover identity. People would find it strange in the future if they recognized you from OTS, but that you hadn't attended graduation. But the graduation ceremony has been pushed back a couple weeks later than usual, with the excuse of an overhaul of the assembly hall's electrical systems."

"So..." Hawk said, "everyone in our graduating class will have their graduation delayed, just so we can be there?"

"That's right." Minho nodded. "Why, do you feel bad about that?"

Hawk grinned. "Hell no. I think it's pretty great."

Minho smiled, amused. "This journey will be your final module of OTS. You'll spend about three weeks on Jamestown, visit a PAC station, and get a feel for living in space. It's very different than living planetside. Some people can't handle it. If one of you can't, now's the time that we need to know about it."

"Like what?" Hawk asked. "Getting space sick?"

Minho shook his head. "Outside of performing extreme maneuvers the inertial dampeners can't handle, or executing zero-g maneuvers, space sickness really doesn't exist anymore. It's a misnomer. What people mean when they say 'space sick' is an issue of the inner ear in relation to artificial gravity. But that's easy enough to handle with a simple dermal injection. Every PAC ship is required to have it in their medical supplies."

"So what would the problem with living in space be?" Peregrine asked. "Claustrophobia?"

Minho tilted his head to one side. "That's part of it.. Most people are okay with the confines of a ship for a short amount of time. But after a little while, they start to get edgy. Part of it is the tight space, part of it is that there's not much between you and instant death in the vacuum of space. That weighs on some people. And while some people can handle a few weeks on a ship to get from here to there, others can get really depressed living in space long term. No sunlight, no fresh air, a feeling of being isolated. A lot of people aren't cut out to live in space."

"But that would be a deal-breaker for us," Raptor guessed. "Because we'll be expected to go wherever, whenever."

"You got it." Minho nodded. "And since you don't know until you try it, here we are."

"So we'll be in space the full four months?" Fallon asked.

"You might go planetside somewhere, if Admiral Krazinski orders it, but you wouldn't stay there long. Why, is that a problem?"

"Nope. I'm ready to put in coordinates to Jamestown and get underway right now."

Minho smiled. "Then by all means, let's get going."

FALLON LOVED BEING IN SPACE.

Yes, the recirculated air lacked a certain freshness. Or maybe it had too much freshness. Something about it was just different. There was an almost antiseptic quality to it, like the smell of a hospital.

And yes, the view sucked. At first, looking out the porthole and straight into space had been thrilling. Fallon had had few opportunities to travel away from Earth, and she'd never gone beyond the Terran system. But after a week, she began to feel the expanse of blackness boring.

After a month, she longed for a little sunlight or a view of something. Anything. Even a parking lot.

But she hadn't expected this to be easy. She was fine.

She'd expected Hawk to have some issues with the tight confines, given his large size, but he didn't seem to mind at all. He didn't mind the lack of view either, and had told her that she was a dumbass for letting it bother her.

After that, she kept such conversations limited to Peregrine and Raptor.

Both of them felt similarly to her, though Raptor, surprisingly, had the strongest reaction to the artificial lighting and lack of sun.

He'd gotten sick the first week.

At first, he seemed a little pale and tired, like he just hadn't slept well. But then he started feeling terribly nauseated.

"Photostimulation adjustment," Minho had explained sympathetically. "It's relatively rare. Most people's bodies accept the artificial light and the way the ship cycles through brighter and darker periods throughout a day. A small group of people find that their bodies don't process the artificial light like it would natural light. It's very treatable, though."

Raptor spent the rest of the voyage resting in a techbed. The ship's infirmary hardly qualified to be called even a mini-medbay. Mostly, it was just a single techbed. But Minho assured them that with daily photostimution therapy, his body would begin to process artificial light as it would natural light. By the time they arrived at Jamestown, he should be just fine.

Fallon enjoyed piloting the ship less than she had expected. It had been made so that it could be flown with minimal pilot skills. Its auto-pilot was also the most advanced she'd ever seen, by light years. A wounded operative could get home even if unconscious.

Provided the operative lived long enough to arrive, of course.

Minho briefed them on items like shaker charges, which were like data bombs that a ship threw at another, to give an opponent a hard shake and steal information from their systems. He taught her how to create a "slip" for important items like identification documents that she didn't want anyone to find.

She might, he told her, travel with a dozen sets of identification credentials at once. And she'd need to hide them someplace that even someone searching for hidden things couldn't sniff out.

It was enlightening, learning about these tools and methodologies.

"You'll never read or hear about it," Minho said one day during a session, "but splitters were a critical piece of the treaty that created the PAC. At that time, people were using devices that were implanted into a person's brain, and used electrical induction to tap into their memories and relay them in visual form, to the person controlling the splitter."

"Sounds like a very useful tool for getting critical data," Peregrine said.

"Sure," Minho said. "And maybe you don't even mind that the person's brain will basically disintegrate within a couple weeks. Splitters are a death sentence, but also a torture device. I've had to kill people, but I can't imagine doing it that way. It's just not..." He shook his head. "It's the worst thing I can think of."

"So they're prohibited in the PAC membership treaty?" Raptor asked.

Minho nodded. "Yep. And the use of splitters led to adding other items to the treaty, too. Agreements that brain augmentation wouldn't be used. No implantation of intelligence or memory hardware, nothing that artificially augments the capacity of a brain."

"What about medical issues, like with brain trauma?" Raptor asked.

"There are technologies allowed for that treatment, but the emphasis is on tissue repair and regeneration, and the eventual removal of all hardware if possible. Doctors take those situations very seriously. The past use of splitters and brain augmentation showed them exactly how horrific such things can be, even when intended to be a therapeutic tool."

It was a sobering concept. Fallon was glad that treaties had been put into place to prevent such atrocities. The idea of anyone tampering with or augmenting her own brain sounded like a living nightmare.

By the time they arrived at Jamestown, she'd learned some hard truths about the ugly side of maintaining an alliance.

No doubt she'd only just begun to see the reality.

9

JAMESTOWN WAS BEAUTIFUL.
Fallon had seen still images of it on the voicecom, of course. She'd even spent hours studying it via holo-vids. She had circled around the projection, studying it from every angle.
Nothing compared to seeing the real thing, though, hovering in space.
It was shaped somewhat like a short, wide bowl, with a beautiful symmetry that made the topmost and lowermost points somewhat tapered inward but aligned with one another. All of Jamestown's curves were smooth but strong and elegant. It could have been constructed just that year, it was so well-maintained. A series of docking ports lined the entire exterior perimeter, with most of them being concentrated in the middle deck.
She knew from her extensive reading and from Minho's description, that Deck 8, right in the center, served as the hub of most things that occurred on Jamestown. And she aimed the little rocket-like ship she currently commanded right at the docking port on Deck 8.
Jamestown.

As she got closer, her heart swelled. This was what she'd been aiming for all these years. Her chance to come here, be a part of this, and protect the alliance.

She'd do whatever it took to make sure no one harmed it. That deep urge drowned out everything else. Her past, her future, even her current personal life—none of it compared to the thing that was so much bigger than herself. She felt like she'd been born for the alliance and its headquarters, Jamestown.

As she guided the ship to the docking clamps and began the docking procedure, she knew she'd never forget this moment.

Fallon tried not to gawk. She really did. She held it together pretty well as Minho guided them through corridors, across a common area, and into the administrative offices.

Even at the academy and OTS, she'd never seen so many officers. Ensigns, lieutenants, commanders, captains, and admirals were everywhere. PAC contractors, too, went about their business with efficiency.

Then they reached the bridge, and Fallon had to remind herself to keep her jaw from dropping.

Here it was. The actual bridge—or ops control, as a station's bridge was called—of Jamestown. It had science stations, a large viewscreen in the front, and command chairs, as would a large ship.

The captain in command at the moment took no notice of them at all. Nor should she. They were little more than official sightseers at the moment.

But soon, Fallon promised herself, she'd do something useful for the PAC. Something that made her truly belong here, even if the commanding officers never recognized her name or face.

She didn't care about recognition. She just wanted to be useful.

Minho quietly led them out after a good but brief look at ops control. Then he led them farther and farther into a labyrinth of offices. The deeper into the warren they went, the fewer faces they saw. Finally, they opened a door and saw a familiar face.

"About time," Admiral Krazinski said as they made their bows. "I've been looking forward to this. How do you like Jamestown?"

Fallon expected Raptor, as their ambassador of friendly charisma, would answer. He didn't, though. Right. She was the leader. She should answer for her team.

"It's even better than I'd imagined it, sir." She said it with pure sincerity and no flattery whatsoever.

"Glad to hear it. And how was the trip? Anyone try to murder a teammate? Wouldn't be the first time." Krazinski said easily, smiling as if it were a joke, but she was pretty sure he wasn't kidding.

"Ah, no," she said. "Hawk once threatened to eat everything and leave us to starve, but it didn't happen."

Hawk sent her a look of stunned outrage. He apparently hadn't expected her to say something so frank to the admiral.

She stifled a giggle.

"Well, I'm glad to hear it," Krazinski said. "I'm only sorry that you won't be here longer. A shame we have to keep up appearances by having you attend graduation, but covert ops is sometimes as inconvenient as it could possibly ever be." He smiled. "I won't keep you. I'm sure you're eager to check out your quarters and do some exploring. First, though, I want to introduce you to the other admiral you'll be working with while you're here."

Nothing happened.

"Scrap," Krazinski said with a self-deprecating gesture. "I thought I'd timed that perfectly. I guess he's a little farther down the corridor than I thought."

A moment later, the doors opened and Fallon saw a second familiar face. This one was a surprise, though.

Krazinski said, "This is Admiral Colb. He's my counterpart in Blackout, so we share equal position, though you're my team. He has his own teams to run. I wish Admiral Erickson were on the station at the moment, but you'll have to meet him next time."

Fallon stared at Colb long after giving him a deep bow. Should she pretend not to know him? She didn't know the protocol for meeting someone she'd known since childhood. She'd grown up calling him Uncle Masumi, he was so close to her family. He and his wife Andra weren't blood, but they might as well have been.

He'd even sponsored her application to the academy.

Uncle Masumi was in Blackout.

Did her father know about that? No, surely he didn't.

She waited to see what he would do.

"There she is," Colb said. "I told you she'd impress you, didn't I?"

Krazinski chuckled. "You did. And I have to admit, I made myself a particularly harsh critic just to make up for it. But even so, I've been greatly pleased with the progress of Avian Unit. You raised her well."

Her team stared at her, as did Minho.

She'd have some explaining to do later.

Colb laughed. "I did no such thing. Her parents did all the raising. I just spoiled her a little along the way and encouraged her combat skills."

He smiled at her. "How are you, Fallon?"

He knew her by a different name, of course, but even though he was willing to acknowledge their past relationship, she was certain he'd never divulge her birth name.

"Excellent, thank you, Admiral. Minho's taking good care of us."

Colb nodded. "As I'd expect. He was once the rising star that your team now is. He's one of our very finest."

He'd been a rising star, just as they were now? Fallon looked at Minho, wondering what that meant, since his team was now dead.

She didn't like the implication.

"Thank you, sir." Minho bowed.

Krazinski waved toward the door. "Go show them around. Feed them. Report back tomorrow at the beginning of first rotation."

"Yes, sir."

After another round of bows, Minho led them back out the labyrinth of offices.

As soon as they made it out into a common area, Hawk punched her shoulder. For him, it was a light bap, but it still hurt.

"What was up with that? You grew up with that guy?" Hawk demanded.

The others looked no less eager for answers.

"He's a friend of my family. Close friend."

"So he knows your family and your birth name and...everything." Raptor spoke softly to avoid being overheard, but she heard a lot of thought going on behind his words.

No doubt he was thinking that Colb knew things about her that Raptor never would.

It was no doubt a strange revelation for him, given their closeness.

"I'm really not sure what to make of that," he admitted.

"Me neither," Minho said. "I can't decide if that gives you an advantage somehow, or a serious, serious disadvantage."

She hadn't thought of it that way. "Neither, I hope. He's an admiral. Surely he's learned to be completely unbiased and neutral when it comes to work matters."

"True," Minho admitted.

"Is it a security breach, though," Peregrine wondered. "He knows your background. Things that aren't even in your record.

Someone could use those details against you. Or him. Or PAC command."

"I know the same things about him." She regretted the words as soon as she said them, and they didn't clarify the situation, but made things far more murky. She, a nobody, knew critical things about an admiral.

That didn't seem good for her.

The others were subtle enough not to say it, but she didn't like it. At all.

Hawk lacked subtlety. "Sucks for you."

She sighed.

"Are you guys hungry?" Minho asked, probably trying to change the subject and take the focus away from her.

Silently, she thanked him.

"Starved," Hawk said.

Food was the ideal way to distract him.

"I'll take you to the boardwalk. All PAC stations have one. All the restaurants and shops are there."

That certainly piqued Fallon's interest. The food would no doubt be varied and tasty, but what shops would a PAC station have?

Everything people needed, she supposed. It wasn't like people could just take a taxi to the next town over to get something.

Funny. She'd never really thought about the incidentals of day-to-day life on a station in quite that way.

Did it get boring? There were thousands of people living and working on Jamestown, but they had to get tired of one another, and probably of their environs. What did they do when they felt that way?

She had three weeks to find out.

She wished it could be longer.

The boardwalk was a study in organized chaos. The shops and restaurants were neatly arranged at regular intervals, impeccably tidy, but each had its own personality.

A clothing shop had bright colors and fashions Fallon had never seen. The door to a massage therapy shop opened as Fallon walked by, emitting a faint scent of rosemary.

Some shopkeeps and restaurateurs stood outside their shops, greeting people, while others did not. Some shops had large signs, while others went entirely unmarked.

All of it was terribly interesting, and she wanted to visit them all.

For the moment, they all selected their dinners and rejoined one another at a table on the boardwalk. Minho said the larger restaurants had interior seating, but they'd agreed that they'd rather people-watch on the boardwalk.

She was curious about all the people. From the admiral who strode by, head high and shoulders back to the janitorial staff who whisked by, constantly keeping everything clean and organized—every person interested her. What had brought them here, and what did they do every day?

How long had they been there, and did they like it?

As they ate, Minho described many of the routine daily operations. "You'll be assigned storage lockers on the lowest level. They're highly secure, so you can store anything there."

"So...will this be our home base?" Raptor asked.

Minho looked conflicted, like he didn't know quite how to answer that. "You won't have a home base. You'll travel to the ends of the PAC zone, when necessary. If an assignment means staying in one place for a year, that's what you'll do. Most are shorter, but anything's possible. So you'll stay on the move. Given your department, that means you'll get storage here. It has the advantage of high security, and a fairly central location in the PAC zone."

What would it be like not to have a home? Would that get old after a while? She kept the question to herself because she suspected that it was something each person had to experience to decide what they thought about it.

Some things, she would have to simply learn by doing.

"Will we at least get a cool ship?" Hawk asked. "One with weapons, I mean."

Minho smiled. "Sometimes. You'll be assigned whatever is needed for the particular mission. Don't be too eager to get into a space battle, though. If that happens, it means everything has pretty much gone to scrap, and you'll be lucky if you don't join the slag heap with your ship."

"Great pep talk. Really warmed my heart. Thanks." Hawk saluted Minho with his beverage.

"Reality." Minho shrugged. "Get used to it. You'll see more and more of it as you go along."

After eating, they looked around the shops, then Minho showed them some of the more basic parts of the station. They took a lift down to the storage area, then had a quick look at engineering.

Fallon wondered what the officers on duty thought of the tour. Did they think Fallon and her team were newly stationed to Jamestown or here for training or what?

They probably had a lot of people circulating through here this way, she supposed. There was no particular reason for Avian Unit and Minho to be noticed.

As long as they did their job well, they would *never* be noticed. No one knew about Minho's team and what they'd given up to serve the PAC. They had simply disappeared into the ether when they'd died. The same would happen to Avian Unit, outside a few individuals on the inside of PAC intelligence, regardless of whether or not they survived their years of service.

That was just fine with Fallon. She didn't want to be known.

At the end of the tour, Minho returned them to the boardwalk. "I have some things to take care of. Do you want me to walk you back to your quarters, or would you rather look around some more? You have access to all common areas, just none of the duty stations."

Fallon hadn't finally arrived at Jamestown to hang out in borrowed quarters and watch holo-vids. "I'd rather remain here." The others quickly agreed.

After Minho left, Hawk said, "I don't know about you guys, but I'm going to continue my tour of the station's culinary offerings."

"How can you eat again so soon?" Raptor asked in amazement. "You ate enough for three people earlier."

"Three lame people," Hawk scoffed. He jutted out a hip and put his hands at his waist. "It takes a lot to maintain all this."

Fallon and Raptor snickered.

"Right. Enjoy. We'll catch up to you later," Fallon said.

Peregrine watched Hawk go, with her own understated expression of amusement. "Actually, I'm a bit tired. I think I'll go to my quarters and rest. There's no telling what they'll do—wake us up in the middle of the night or what. I might as well be ready for anything."

"Good plan. You know the way?" Fallon asked.

"Sure. See you."

That left Fallon and Raptor to take in the sights of Jamestown. "Funny how we still call it night," she mused. "Even though there's no night out here. Just artificially segmented time periods."

"What would we do otherwise?" Raptor wondered. "Time would just stretch out into chaos with no form or function."

"No, of course we have to simulate days, since our bodies work on a daily cycle. I mean, why not call it a sleep cycle or an awake cycle or something?"

Raptor shrugged. "Maybe people do. Some grow up on space stations. To them, going to a planet is an oddity. What do you think that's like? They must have an entirely different perspective on life."

"I can't imagine that," she admitted.

"Neither can I. But we'll have to figure it out, because we need to be able to understand how people think. You know, so we can pretend to be one of them." He made his eyes big and clownishly sneaky.

She ignored his silliness. Sometimes it was the only thing to do. "What's your plan? I want to check out the commissary to see what people here like to stock in their kitchens. Then maybe get an ice cream."

"You noticed the ice cream place, too?" he asked. "I was kind of thinking about checking it out."

"Yep. Let's go."

Fallon wasn't sure what she expected of her time on Jamestown. After all, Minho had explained this trip as a deep-space tolerance test. Though the thrill of being on Jamestown didn't dim, it did get buried under paperwork.

Boring, drudging paperwork.

Another anachronistic phrase, since no paper products were involved. Sometimes people said "forms" or "recordkeeping" but mostly people just used the old, inaccurate phrase.

Funny how some words stuck around long after their actual meaning no longer existed.

"It's important to keep your records accurate," Minho said. "You're creating the illusion of an entire life. If there's a missing performance appraisal or acquisitions request, it might stick out. If it sticks out, it could get flagged. If it gets flagged, someone's going to specifically examine that person's profile. We don't want that. So keep your paperwork pristine."

More usefully, but no more excitingly, they learned the protocol demands of working while undercover. Who to report to. Who not to report to. How to get a direct line to Krazinski. Exactly what they could and couldn't divulge to whom about both their long-term cover identities—those of Emiko, Drew, Olag, and Poppy—and the short-term ones that they'd be assigned as needed.

It was a lot of protocol, and sometimes it seemed to conflict, but it was critical they never made a single mistake.

After two weeks of it, though, she felt better prepared for the grind of the details of working in covert ops. Much of it, no doubt, would be dull. Traveling from one place to another. Watching. Waiting. Doing paperwork.

She suspected this was another test of their resolve and compatibility.

When they arrived within the labyrinth of Krazinski's offices for another day of drudgery, he surprised them.

"Change of plans," he announced. "You're going to go on a brief mission. From there, you'll return to Earth to graduate OTS. The timing works out perfectly, since the target destination of the mission is only a very minor detour on your way back."

Fallon, like her teammates, perked up but tried not to show it. Of the four of them, Hawk failed the most miserably. He had tolerated the paperwork well enough, but with less stoicism than the rest of them.

"What's the mission?" Hawk asked.

Krazinski smiled. "You'll be operating on a need-to-know basis. That is, you'll know what you need to know when you need to know it."

They waited, watching him.

"For now, all you need to know is that you'll be posing as traders, looking for a buyer for your ship."

"Uh." Raptor rubbed at the back of his neck. "The same ship that we'll need to get back to Earth?"

"That's the one," the admiral agreed.

"Won't we kind of need that?" Raptor asked.

"Yes, indeed." The admiral said no more.

Right. Need to know. Fallon guessed they didn't need to know just yet, and that they had to get accustomed to working with limited information.

Okay.

She was ready.

10

"WHAT DO you think this mission is really about?" Raptor asked. He'd ducked into her quarters after they'd all retired for the evening to rest up for the next day.

She shrugged, sitting on the floor in front of the couch with her back resting against its front. "We won't know until after we do it, and maybe we won't know then, either."

"You think it'll be weird to live like that?" He sprawled sideways on the couch, taking up its entire length. His feet lay somewhere behind her head. "Just doing what we're told, even if it's something extreme, purely because we've been given orders? Then never knowing why."

"I'm sure sometimes we'll know the purpose. But not knowing only matters if we don't trust the source of our orders."

He nodded slowly. "True. As long as we continue to trust the one giving us orders, we'll be working on the faith that what we're doing is for the greater good of the PAC."

"Exactly. And someday, when we're admirals, we'll depend on young dummies like us to do the grunt work, too."

He laughed. "I like how little you think of us."

"It's all perspective."

He nudged her in the shoulder with his toe. "Why do you sit like that, by the way? There's a perfectly good couch right here."

"I don't know. I've always liked it. Maybe it's an innate instinct to protect my head by keeping it low. Don't be a target, you know?"

He gave her a gentle shove on the back of her head with his foot. "Yeah, somehow I doubt it. You're not that paranoid."

"Maybe I am, and I'm just really good at hiding it."

"Nope. Not buying it. Try again."

"I'm your team leader," she retorted. "I could just order your ass out of here. I don't owe you explanations."

"Oh, nice," he said. "You're getting a head start on your admiralty. I like it."

They grinned at each other.

"What station do you think we'll be going to?" she asked.

"There's only one big one between us and Earth. But maybe the admiral will throw us a loop by taking us farther out of our way, or having us stop at some dinky little outpost."

"I thought about that, too," he admitted. "We'll just have to wait and see."

"And get used to waiting and seeing," she added.

"Yep. This is our life now."

The faux bleak tone of his voice made her laugh. "You should go back to your quarters. You've been here a while now, and we don't want to give people ideas."

"You think they're watching?" he asked.

"Oh yeah. I think they are. I think they've been watching us since we first stepped foot on the academy's campus."

"So then they'd know everything there is to know," he concluded. "No point in trying to hide it."

"On the contrary," she said. "If we're ever going to have anything to ourselves, anything that's truly ours and not theirs to know, we have to be extra careful to keep it safe."

He blinked at her. "Huh. I guess I'll go back to my quarters and ponder that. I mean, are you being an amazing leader right now, or should I report you for mental insubordination?"

"That's not a thing."

"Right. Okay." He swung his feet around and stood, and in the processing of doing so, he hit her in the head again with his foot. Seemingly by accident, but she knew better by his playful grin.

"You'd better hurry up before I pick you up and throw you into the corridor," she warned. "Then they'll really have something to keep in their super-extra-secret records on us."

"I'm going, I'm going. Good night, fearless leader."

She wished she had something to throw at his back as he made for the door.

"Good night," she laughed.

The door closed, but she was still smiling.

"Dragonfire Station." Fallon peered out the porthole so she could get a look at it with her own eyes.

It was nothing like Jamestown. It was long and pointed, with the bulk of the station located at the top. Most notably, it had gotten its name from the nebula that surrounded it. At a distance, it did kind of look like a mythical dragon had breathed fire at the station.

Though it was just a station, and not the command headquarters of the PAC, it had its own charm.

They docked and went through a docking bay to enter the station directly on its boardwalk.

Fallon rooted herself in her cover identity. She was a trader named Sella. She now had long brown hair and she no longer looked Japanese. Peregrine had short, silvery-white hair with purple streaks and though she still looked human, she looked older and a little overweight.

Hawk was now a Rescan, and Raptor had dark hair, blue eyes, and spoke with a bit of a lisp.

They were all someone else.

Except for Minho.

"You've learned everything you need to know for this. I'm not coming with you," he'd said.

Instead, he remained on the ship.

For Fallon and her team, it was their first time traveling with false credentials and committing completely to alter egos.

As she emerged into the bustle of activity on board the station, she wasn't sure whether to be excited or nervous, so she aimed for excited.

Dragonfire Station's boardwalk had some similarities to that of Jamestown. Fallon saw shops and stores and people, but the people seemed slightly more relaxed. More like they were at home compared to being at work. She saw more civilians, too. Contractors and shopkeeps and people who were just visiting. Dragonfire was a waypoint for travelers and a hub of trade activity.

The number of children she saw surprised her. Small ones with their parents and adolescents hanging around in groups.

Dragonfire had a lot of families on board, apparently.

People paid Avian Unit little attention. They must have seen lots of traders coming and going. That was good. It meant that if they were careful, they could go about their business without any notice.

She hoped that was how it went.

Krazinski had given them orders to go to a trader's shop. The man in question, a Rescan, was under suspicion of smuggling. Not because there had ever been any proof, the admiral had said, but because there was an absolute absence of proof.

Which was suspicious.

Avian Unit's mission was to engage in trade negotiations for their ship. It would allow PAC command to see if the man had the kind of internal trading network to make such a sale and, more importantly, allow Fallon and her team to install a bug in his shop so they could do some passive surveillance.

Fallon had never engaged in trade negotiations for a huge purchase before, and she'd certainly never done so with the intention of not completing a deal. She wasn't going to let that bother her, though.

Finding the shop was easy. They headed to the right and kept going until they saw it. With a silent glance at her team, they entered.

It wasn't what she'd expected. The well-kept shop had a variety of goods, from art to tabletop games to ribbons.

She didn't know what the ribbons would be for. Decoration? Hair?

Everything was artfully displayed and impeccably tidy. She smelled something too. Something faintly woody and pleasant.

It sure didn't feel like the shop of a cutthroat smuggler.

Maybe that was the point.

"Well, hello, four new faces." A middle-aged man, presumably their target, approached them with a deferential posture. He didn't bow, and there was no reason he should. He wasn't an officer and they weren't either, by all appearances. Etiquette only required him to bow in formal situations with commissioned PAC officers.

"What can I do for you?" He smiled benignly.

He seemed like anything but a big-time dealer, whether he was a smuggler or not.

Fallon had assigned Hawk to take the lead position. He was huge, intimidating, and appeared to be a Rescan trader. That alone would give him at least a little credibility.

Hawk said, "Are you Cabot Layne? We were told we could talk to you. We're looking to sell our ship."

The man's eyebrows rose. "A referral? How flattering. But as you can see, I hardly have room in here for a ship." He opened his hands in a gesture that indicated the shop.

"We were told you can broker outside sales."

Layne paused. "Occasionally. I mean, if I happen to know someone who's looking for something and I can put them in touch with it. But a ship is a pretty big expenditure. I don't know if anyone I know is in the market."

"Docking Bay 6," Hawk said. "Here are the specs." He pushed an infoboard at Layne.

Fallon held her breath. They needed negotiations to go on long enough to present them with an opportunity to install the bug. If Layne dismissed them outright, they'd be out of luck.

As if she didn't care about the negotiations, she wandered away and started perusing the artwork with a frown.

"That's a very interesting ship," Layne said behind her. "You don't see too many of those. Given its rarity, I could put word out that it's on the market and see if there's any interest. I really can't promise anything, though."

"How long do you need?" Hawk asked.

"Give me a day. Anyone who can't be bothered to answer in that period of time isn't truly interested anyway."

"Fine." Hawk turned to go.

"While you're here," Layne said, "is there anything you're in need of? I have a wide variety of inventory."

Hawk shook his head and started to decline, but Fallon spoke up. "What's your price on this piece?"

She stood in front of a small stone sculpture.

Layne moved to join her. "That's a very interesting piece. You have quite an eye for art, I can tell. Because of its rarity, I have it priced at fifty thousand cubics. Since I can see what a connoisseur you are, I'll sacrifice it for forty-five."

She smirked. "It's second-century. It's not worth a credit more than twenty thousand."

His gaze sharpened, and she saw a hint of a smile behind his obsequious expression.

"It's clearly first-century," he gently argued. "Look at the coloration of the stone at the base. There's just a bit of pink. I can get you a color spectrometer, if you like."

A challenge. He'd thrown a proverbial gauntlet at her.

"No need," she said curtly. "There is indeed a hint of pink but that's not because of the type of stone used. It's color transfer from some other item. Probably not an intentional attempt to pass off second-century art for first-century Atalan art, but it's second-century nonetheless. The giveaway is the porosity of the stone under the base."

"You can't see the base, since it's sitting on it," he pointed out kindly.

"If you flip it, you'll see I'm right." She looked straight into his eyes, unflinching.

A smile spread across his face. "Let's take a look, then."

Carefully, he grasped the sculpture and turned it over.

The stone under the base was full of teeny holes.

"Ah, so you're right. I'm very impressed. You're clearly a high-end art dealer. I only know of one other person who could make such a distinction with plain eyesight." He gave her a respectful nod.

"I'm a dealer of multiple things," she said. "All four of us are. Right now, we're looking to dig up some capital. Do you think you could find some interest in the ship?"

"It's a niche item," he said apologetically, "and I'm assuming you're on a deadline?"

At her nod, he said, "I don't know. If I had a couple of days to work through some channels, I could probably scare up someone who might be interested in it for a collection, but a quick exchange is a lot more iffy."

"I see. We'll be staying on our ship, so if you come up with something, please let us know right away."

"Of course. Is there anything else I can help you with?" He smiled.

There was something about him. He was hiding something beneath his pleasant manner. He was unusually observant, she suspected, and particularly shrewd.

It was probably better to leave before he caught on to them. Hopefully when he called them back, they'd get a chance to plant the bug.

Fallon sent a questioning look to Hawk, who was supposed to be her boss.

Hawk shook his head. "There's nothing else we need. Let's go."

They filed out of the store and said nothing until they made it to the docking bay and closed the doors behind them.

"There's something about that guy. The trader," Peregrine chewed on her thumb.

Raptor nodded. "He's smarter than he lets on."

"I agree," Fallon said.

Hawk turned to her. "How did you know about that carved rock thing? That was pretty slick. He totally believed you were a savvy trader at that point."

"I had downtime on the trip to Jamestown, so I read up on some interstellar history. I read a book on Atalan art." Fallon shrugged.

"Hah," Hawk said. "That's a fortunate choice. I guess studying up paid off."

"It's just luck." Minho stepped through the airlock to join them in the docking bay. "Sometimes luck breaks your way, and sometimes it does anything but. All you can do is roll with what you get. So it went well?"

They relayed the experience to him, and though he nodded, he offered no advice.

"What will you do while you wait?" he asked.

Fallon had wondered that too. "Sightseeing on the station

seems out of character for our identities. It seems like the best choice is to lay low here, where we're least likely to get in our own way."

Minho nodded again, and remained silent.

Apparently, he was going to give them no guidance at all.

"So when will you drop the bug?" he asked.

"Layne will get back to us at some point, either because he does or does not have information," Fallon said. "I'll make sure we meet in person, in his shop, to discuss it. It will have to be then. Maybe we can convince him to check his storeroom for something, or maybe we'll need to employ a distraction. We'll have different options ready."

She tried to sound completely confident.

"Okay, then. Sounds like you've got it handled." Minho's expression didn't suggest whether he thought she was going about this right or doing it all wrong.

Would he pull her back if she was about to tank, or would he let her go through with it as a learning experience?

She wished she knew.

The silence went on a beat too long and Hawk got impatient. "Okay, this is boring. I'm going to go make myself a sandwich. Unless there's any chance of getting some food delivered to us from the boardwalk."

He looked from one of them to the next. "No?"

He shrugged and boarded the ship.

LAYNE'S CALL came a mere twelve hours later. Fallon didn't answer it, even though she was itching to. She let him leave her a message, then she checked it.

Let's talk, it said. *Come to my shop.*

Should they respond immediately? Maybe that would seem too eager. Being too eager would give him an advantage.

But then, maybe giving him an advantage would make him complacent and more likely to allow them to get into a position to plant the bug.

It wasn't tough to do. One of them simply had to slip it somewhere unnoticeable and activate it. Given that small devices were Peregrine's specialty, she'd assigned that duty to her.

That left it to Fallon and the others to keep Layne busy.

She sent the other three ahead of her. By arriving late, maybe she'd be a distraction. Or maybe they'd need to go bigger, with one of the potential diversionary tactics they'd rehearsed.

After waiting ten minutes, she went to join the others at Layne's shop. She saw them standing near the back of the store, at the counter.

She approached on the opposite side from Peregrine, giving her partner as much room as she could to operate.

"...interested buyer, but without the capital right now. Are you able to wait two weeks?" Layne was saying.

Hawk shook his head. "Too late. We need to be somewhere."

"Where's that?" Layne asked.

Hawk narrowed his eyes suspiciously.

Layne held up his hands apologetically. "I'm not prying. I do a lot of arranging cargo delivery. I just thought that if you were going the right way anyway, we might be able to arrange something."

"But no ship?" Fallon asked, drawing attention to her.

"No, not at this time, as I was explaining to your colleagues. Not a lot of people want a ship without weapons, no matter how fast it is. It's too much money tied up in something that can't defend itself."

"Except for running away," Hawk said. "Try approaching that ship and getting within weapons range. Not much chance."

"Sounds like you're fond of it," Layne said.

"It's a great ship," Hawk said. "I don't really want to lose it. But I hate to miss an opportunity even more." He shrugged.

Layne nodded. "I understand. I wish I could help you out with this one, but I'm afraid not."

So that was that. Fallon was pretty certain Peregrine hadn't planted the bug yet, so now what?

She'd arranged signals for her team to pick up to cue the beginning of one of their diversions. But Layne was standing there, staring right at them, and there was no reason for them to linger.

Scrap.

She'd have to figure something else out.

"I guess we'll be going then," Hawk said.

"Of course. Good luck in your future endeavors."

"You too," Hawk answered.

Back at the ship, Fallon struggled with her frustration. They'd had multiple plans. How had none of them been useful? They'd just stood there, like idiots, leaving before they'd gotten the job done.

Judging from her teammates' expressions and body language, they didn't feel any better about it than she did.

"Now what?" Hawk asked.

"We should have kept one of us aside," Fallon said aloud. "Someone who wasn't apparently a part of our group who could have come in and been a distraction. Making ourselves seem more legit by having more members wasn't the way to go."

"Apparently not," Raptor agreed.

Fallon pulled off her wig and turned to Peregrine. "Make me someone else."

"Who?" Peregrine asked.

Fallon thought quickly. Who would be the most trustworthy person? She wanted to find the right mix of inconspicuous and nonthreatening. "A woman around fifty years old. A PAC captain. Can you do that?"

No one would take notice of yet another captain making a brief visit.

"I can do the makeup, and we have the uniform, but do you have the insignia? And what if someone sees you? Impersonating an officer, or an officer of a higher rank, is a serious offense."

"I'll have to be convincing then," Fallon said. "I'll talk to Minho about the insignia."

She checked the time. "We'll have to wait until morning. He'll be closing up shop now."

"I'll put in a request to undock in the morning," Raptor said. "So it won't look strange that we're still here."

"Good. We'll make this work." She only hoped Minho could help her with the insignia.

"Sure," Minho said. He retreated into his quarters and came out a minute later with a captain's insignia. "Here."

She stared at him. "Why do you have that?"

He shrugged. "Sometimes things come up. Don't they?"

She smiled. "Yeah. Apparently so. I guess I'll have to plan on that in the future."

"Yep." He didn't say anything else and didn't invite her in.

"Are we...doing okay?" she ventured.

"Fine, except you haven't gotten the job done."

"But this plan makes sense?"

He shrugged. "Sometimes the best plans don't work. Sometimes the worst plans do. All that matters is getting the job done. So make sure you do."

"Right. Okay." His chilly response surprised her a little. She turned away. "Good night."

"Hang on," he said. "I want you to succeed, and I do care. But the next time you do this, I probably won't be along to ask for advice. You need to do this on your own, without feedback. Find a way to get the job done and do it. Okay?"

"Yeah. Okay. Thanks."

When she got to her cabin, she put the insignia in a drawer. Tomorrow she'd become a captain, for just a little while.

PEREGRINE GAVE Fallon some last-minute pointers before she went back to Layne's shop.

"Remember, you're fifty. Slow your movements. Be deliberate. And watch your voice. Think about speaking from the base of your throat. Keep plenty of air in your lungs, don't speak too fast, and take a breath just before you start a sentence."

"Right." Fallon smoothed her hand over her waistband. The bug was inside.

"You'll do great," Peregrine assured her. "You're going to nail this, and then we're going to go graduate OTS. And *then* we're going to make the hairy man-beast take us out for drinks and dinner, to make up for all the food he stole from us."

Fallon smiled. "I like that plan. Okay. Here I go."

She left the ship, then stepped out onto the boardwalk. She wanted to look around to see if anyone noticed her coming out of the docking bay, but suppressed the urge. She kept her eyes forward, her stride steady, and just a touch slower than usual, and her expression serious.

Nobody wanted to bother a captain who had something to deal with.

She entered Layne's shop, noting that a couple of small artworks had been replaced with other items. Had he made sales, or did he just like to change out his display items now and then?

"Hello." Just as he had before, Layne approached, looking pleasant and helpful. He bowed, and Fallon was reminded of her pretend rank of captain. He hadn't strictly needed to bow, but he'd chosen to do so, all the same, as a show of respect.

She kept her words measured and imagined them coming

from her neck. "Hello. I was hoping you could help me find a gift."

"I'm certain I could. Did you have something particular in mind?"

"Not really. A colleague's son was just accepted into the academy and I wanted to send something nice, but I don't know what kids that age like."

"Ah, of course. Were you hoping for something practical, or something with a bit of luxury?"

"Practical. I'm sure he won't have much use for fancy things once he starts moving around."

"An excellent point. Practical gifts are often the best, aren't they?" Layne smiled conspiratorially. "Let's see. Ah. I know just the thing. It's in the back. Would you like some tea?"

Yes! Fallon fought to maintain her composure. She wanted him to go immediately, but would accepting some tea make her seem more normal and less likely to arouse suspicion?

No, she decided. Captains were busy. She had no reason to accept tea from a man who didn't know her. No doubt he was being polite in the interest of buttering her up as a customer.

"No, thank you. I have a meeting to get to before my ship departs."

"Of course. I won't be long at all. Please have a look around while you wait. You never know when you'll see something that calls to you."

She smiled and nodded.

She approached a display of decorative teapots and pretended to study them. As soon as he disappeared into the back, she bolted across the shop. She'd already cased the place. She couldn't leave the bug on a shelf or inside a vase. He'd find it if he moved his inventory around. She had to put it under the counter, where he wouldn't look. Hopefully not for a long, long time.

She glanced at the door, hoping no one would come in. If

they did, she'd claim that she needed to use the voicecom. No one would find it amiss that an officer in her fifties preferred not to use the tiny screen on her comport.

Running her hand over the counter, she looked for a seam or crease, but it was perfectly smooth. Layne had invested in quality materials.

Okay, underneath, then. There were shelves and cubbyholes. She chose the bottom leftmost one. Pretending to study the voicecom display, she reached for the bug and activated it. She bent slightly and extended her arm to the back of the cubby, behind several boxes of cleansing cloths.

Layne clearly had a penchant for keeping his shop clean.

She installed the bug, then hurried back across the shop and began to admire a really horrible painting. It was like someone had splattered chunks of food on a canvas. It was easily the worst excuse for art Fallon had ever seen.

Layne emerged, carrying a black rectangle. "Do you like that one? Striking, isn't it?"

"You know, I was just thinking it looked like it had been stricken a number of times," she mused.

She paused. Would her character make a joke?

She decided she would.

Layne's eyes widened, then he laughed. "You know what," he said, sounding the most genuine she'd ever heard him, "I hate that thing too. But believe it or not, that artist is very popular right now."

He made a helpless gesture and they both laughed.

"I think your colleague's son would like this." He set the item on the table that sat in the middle of the shop. With a quick gesture, it popped up into a large travel bag. "These are great. Extremely durable material and approved for all PAC interstellar travel. And it doesn't take much space to store in tiny quarters." He pressed on the ends of the bag and it flattened back into a perfect, fairly flat rectangle.

"That's really nice," she said honestly. "Where did that come from?"

"My home planet, of course. All the best things come from Rescissitan." He smiled.

She couldn't help but smile back. There was something about him. She wouldn't trust him for a second, but in spite of his slick demeanor, he was smart and resourceful. She was certain of that.

"How much is it?"

He named a reasonable price.

Would her character haggle over the price? Fallon would. But she decided the captain was too busy to waste time at something like that, especially for something that was reasonable to begin with.

"I'll take it."

He whipped out an infoboard from somewhere, and she transferred credits from the secured account Krazinski had set up for her.

"Is there anything else I can do for you?" he asked.

"No, you've been very helpful. Thank you."

He bowed. More shallowly this time, but it was very respectful to do so, all the same. "My pleasure. I hope the young man enjoys it."

"I'm sure he will." Fallon re-engaged her middle-aged officer walk and carefully retreated down the corridor. She walked as if she were going to pass Docking Bay 6, and she almost did. At the last second, she stepped sideways and in. Hopefully, no one had noticed.

"THAT'S A NICE BAG. I want one." Hawk reached for it.

"Get your own. This one's mine." Fallon held it against her chest.

"So is that it?" Hawk asked Minho. "We're going to Earth now?"

"Going to Earth now." Minho nodded. "Krazinski confirmed that the bug had been deployed, and we're going back now."

"No tricks?" Hawk pressed. "No sudden maneuvers or pirate attacks or stranding us on a desert island somewhere?"

"Well, I mean, we have a little time, if you really want to," Minho said.

"No!" Hawk lowered his voice. "I mean, no thanks. I'm tired of the survival stuff. Ready to move on to real jobs, like this one."

Minho nodded. "Well, enjoy these couple of weeks, then. Once you graduate OTS, specialty school will keep you busy."

Hawk grinned. "I hope you had plenty of food stocked on this boat, because I plan to eat and sleep a whole lot. In fact, I'm going to go get started."

He left with a bounce in his step.

Peregrine and Raptor went with him, which left Fallon alone on the ship's small bridge with Minho.

Once she got the ship undocked and on its way, she turned to him. "Why do I feel like I'm about to get slapped by some surprise?"

He didn't smile. "You're always about to get slapped by some surprise in this job. But there's really nothing intended between here and OTS. So enjoy a little bit of calm while you can."

"Will you be sticking around?" she asked before he left.

"For a while."

Alone on the bridge, she thought about what his answer might mean.

"As an officer of the Planetary Alliance Cooperative, I solemnly vow that I will uphold the standards, treaties, and integrity of the

PAC. I will put my duties and the citizens under my care before myself. I will never abandon my post."

Along with the rest of the graduating class, Fallon recited the end of the officer's pledge.

An air of anticipation went through the assembly hall. A new class of brand-new officers was waiting for the official pronouncement and the beginning of a new future.

Admiral Davies smiled. "As the officer who first inducted you into OTS, I am thrilled to pronounce you all officers. I'm proud of you. Go forth and serve, and may your promotions be frequent and fulfilling."

A cheer went up, quickly turning into a low-level roar of jubilation.

Admiral Davies tried to speak over the ruckus. "I should have mentioned this before—there's a reception with food and drink in the annex. Please stop by so I can congratulate you personally."

For Fallon, the graduation was anti-climactic, but she played along, smiling and patting people on the shoulder in celebration.

"Should we go to the reception?" Peregrine asked in a low voice.

Fallon wanted to get out of the crowd as soon as possible, but free food had been mentioned. She looked to Hawk. "Do you want to go?"

He shrugged. "Nah. I'd have to be polite and pretend to be satisfied with meager portions. Let's go get some real food."

"Right," Raptor said. "I like it. It's your turn to pay, right?"

Hawk looked stricken. "Is it? I wanted to indulge too." He heaved a sigh. "Fine. I'll pay. Don't get used to it, though."

Fallon exchanged a look with Peregrine. Oh yeah, they were definitely going to make sure he felt the pain they felt whenever it was their turn to pay.

Lone Wolf Lowell's was quiet when they arrived. Most people at OTS were attending the reception.

Not Avian Unit. Fallon ordered a bowl of stew, a basket of biscuits, and three drinks for herself.

"Three drinks?" Hawk complained.

"Right," she said, as if he'd just reminded her of something. She picked up her menuboard. "I meant to ask for the premium alcohol, since we're celebrating."

Hawk grumbled and she smiled at him sweetly.

"We should have invited Minho," Raptor said.

"I would have, if he'd been around." Fallon shrugged. "He just kind of shows up when he wants to. I have no way of contacting him."

"Hmm." Raptor pursed his lips. "It does seem like a lopsided relationship. I guess you like him more than he likes you."

She rolled her eyes at his juvenile remark. It was kind of funny, though. Thus far, she and Raptor had kept their relationship low-key and simple. They weren't strictly partners, but they weren't really a couple, either. As long as they didn't define it, it could work.

She hoped so. She liked it this way far more than trying to pretend she had no feelings for him. As far as she was concerned, fighting herself that way was a far bigger distraction than simply going with what felt natural.

Even as she laughed and joked with her team, though, she felt like storm clouds were gathering overhead. She should have heard from Minho. After returning to Earth, he'd disappeared.

Had he gone somewhere? Was something happening?

Was something going to happen to them?

They'd know as soon as Admiral Krazinski wanted them to, and not a second sooner.

All she could do was wait. And order another basket of cheese biscuits. And another drink. Hawk was paying, after all.

11

The day after graduation, all of the brand-new officers began receiving their orders. Fallon observed this mostly as an outsider. She'd made a few friends in the earlier modules, and congratulated them on their assignments, even when those assignments were unfortunate.

New officers tended to get the most undesirable posts. An aging outpost in the middle of nowhere or a stint at a diplomatic specialty school sounded mind-crushingly boring to her. But at least they received news of what was next for them.

No such news came for Avian Unit. No mission, no duty posts, and no news of the promised specialty schools.

As the numbers of people on campus dwindled by the day, Avian Unit remained. Waiting.

With an empty schedule, Fallon upped her workout routine, and pulled her teammates into it, as well.

She knew her partners. They didn't do well with aimless downtime.

Nor did she.

They did weapon training; they ran, and they lifted weights.

Fallon even gave them some knife-throwing lessons, though she could tell that none of them had the knack to ever be great at it.

She kept them busy, and the days passed.

She'd gotten them all to join her for an afternoon run, but she remained alone for her morning one. She'd found that running in the mornings gave her days structure and let her think about the coming day. Getting her thoughts in order was a good thing.

Her running path took her out away from the buildings of the campus and along some nature trails that separated OTS from the city.

The weather was starting to turn cold, which made it easier for her to run farther. Her runs were always shorter in the hot season.

She saw something bounce across the path just ahead and slowed her pace. Cautiously, she approached, looking for whatever it had been. She peered into the brush alongside the path, but saw nothing.

A scratching sound behind her made her turn, and she saw a squirrel skitter up a tree.

"Ah, so it was you." It must have been a fluffy tail she'd noticed.

Rather than going right back to her run she took a moment to watch the little animal run up the tree, perch itself on a branch, and begin furiously cleaning its tail.

"Did you get it dirty?" she asked, chuckling.

"You're talking to woodland creatures now?" A voice from behind her made her spin and move into a defensive stance.

She relaxed when she saw Minho. "What are you doing out here? Just hanging out, in case I decided to go for a run? Seriously, you might have a problem with this need of yours to sneak up on people."

He smiled. "Good to see you too."

She wouldn't admit that she was glad to see him. "Tell me you have our orders. You said we were going to specialty school. Has that changed?"

His smile faded. "No, you're still going. You're not going to like it, though."

Her stomach lurched. "Why?"

"You and your team have different specialties. You're going to different places."

"How different?" she asked. She didn't mind not having the same classes as the others. Her classes at the academy had been quite different from theirs.

"Different planets, split across two systems. You won't be seeing each other until you're done with specialties."

"How long will that be?" she asked.

"Six months."

"That's not very long." It wasn't. She knew it wasn't. So why did it feel like a long time?

Minho looked sympathetic. "I'd like to tell you that you'll stay busy, which you will, and that you'll barely notice the time passing. But you will. Everything Blackout has done to train you this far has been to build you up as a team. Now they're ripping you apart, and that's not going to feel good."

"Why do it?" she asked.

"The obvious reason is that what you need to study happens to be in different places. You'll be doing intensive security. Raptor will be going deep on hacking. Peregrine and Hawk have their own specialized programs, too. But there's more to it. Blackout wants you to feel the separation, and know how much it sucks."

"What, to prove to me that they matter? I already knew that."

Minho nodded. "Yeah. I know. But they want to make sure you know."

She frowned at him, giving him a hard look. "You disapprove."

He rolled one shoulder. "Doesn't matter what I think. The orders are the same. But yeah. Specialty schools are a necessity and if they're in different places, that's just how it is, but I don't like intentional separation. I think it's insulting when you've already proven yourselves."

"But nobody cares what we think, right?" She smiled ruefully.

"Exactly."

"When do we ship out?"

"Tomorrow." His expression softened, and it reminded her of how good-looking he was. "Need help packing?"

She started to say no, but changed her mind. "Sure. It'll really piss Hawk off if I have help and he doesn't."

Laughing, they jogged back to the cabin.

Hawk, Peregrine, and Raptor took the news about as well as she had, but there wasn't time to sit around complaining about it because there was packing to do.

"These are nice," Minho said, poking through her knife collection.

"I said pack those, not invade my privacy."

He grinned. "It's the price you pay for my help."

In actuality, she didn't care if he looked through her things. She didn't own anything embarrassing. She owned very little besides necessary gear.

"You love him, don't you?" Minho sounded sympathetic.

"What? Who?"

He smirked at her. "Come on."

She sighed and sat on the edge of her bed. "So?"

Minho grasped her upper arm briefly in what felt like a gesture of solidarity, then released it. "You've got it under control?"

"Yeah. It's not in the way. It won't get in the way."

He nodded. "If it works, in whatever form you make it work,

then you're lucky. It's something most Blackout officers never get to have."

She felt like he was trying to make a point, so she simply nodded and remained silent.

"But I have two things to say. First, don't let command know about you two. It won't change anything except how they perceive your command decisions. They might see things that aren't there. Preference, maybe. A reluctance to put him in danger."

"That won't happen," she promised. "We'll do our jobs. Nothing will get in the way of that."

"I know. I don't doubt you. That's why I want to tell you something else, too. Something you should never tell command."

"Okay." She steeled herself for whatever truth bomb he was about to drop on her.

"Nobody ever told me this, and I wish they had. There will be times when you're out there, and you have to choose between something bad and something worse. Sometimes there aren't any good options. But if there's an option that's bad and leaves your team dead and a bad choice where they survive—then choose survival. Forget protocol. Save your team. You'll never be whole without them."

He was talking about himself. She could see it in the pain and grief in his face.

She reached out and grasped his upper arm, just like he had hers minutes before.

After a long minute of silence, she said, "I'm guessing you'd get your ass busted if Krazinski or Colb knew you had told me something like that."

He smiled. "Yeah. But I owe it to my team to speak up for yours. We're not as expendable as command sometimes prefers to believe. Not when it comes to one another, anyway."

She nodded.

He patted the bag she'd bought from Layne at Dragonfire

Station and stood. "Your hours are numbered. Go spend them with him. You'll be sorry if you don't."

He was right.

She said, "Thanks for seeing us through OTS. I'm really glad you were here."

"You'll see me again," he promised. "Let's not say any goodbyes. I'm really not a fan of them."

With that, he left.

Fallon didn't bother to sleep that night. She'd be getting on a ship in a matter of hours, and have lots of time to kill before she arrived at her destination—wherever it was.

She'd sleep then.

A crescent of dim light appeared on the wall of Raptor's room, and they watched it grow to engulf the wall then brighten the room.

She squeezed his hand—the one that was wrapped around her.

"It's time, isn't it?" His voice was even, but she knew he wasn't any more eager to say goodbye to her and the others for half a year.

"Yeah. Our transports will be waiting when we get up there."

"Think we'll be able to communicate via the voicecom?" he asked.

"I hope so. But there's no telling. We're on a—"

"Need-to-know basis," he interrupted. "Yeah."

They smiled at each other.

"Just think of it," she said. "Six whole months without Hawk eating your food. It might be the only time like that we ever get."

"True," he agreed. "And you won't be around to tell us what to do, either. So there's that."

She snorted.

He tightened his arms around her, squeezing her tightly, then sighed and let go. "Okay. The sooner we go and get it done, the sooner we'll all be back together. Let's get it done."

She rolled off his bed and stood. "I'll consult with Hawk. I hear he gets shit done."

It was a weak joke, but humor was the best way for them to deal with their separation.

Raptor smiled. "You do that. I'm going to finish packing my socks."

Right. They wouldn't do one last kiss or any promises or declarations. That wasn't the kind of relationship they had. They'd just keep pushing forward, doing what they needed to do.

But, Prelin's ass, was she ever going to miss him.

"DOCKING BAY 23. OKAY." Fallon arrived at her transport alone, carrying the bag she'd bought from Layne. It was remarkably comfortable and had handy little compartments on the sides to stash small items.

After leaving her room, she'd found that Hawk and Peregrine had already left.

They weren't looking forward to saying goodbye either, so they simply hadn't.

Fallon was glad.

She arrived at Docking Bay 23.

Here I go, she thought. *Off to whatever comes next.*

She verified her identity, then stepped through the airlock.

"Looks like a cargo freighter," she said to herself when she got a look at the interior of the ship.

"It is." Minho stepped around a corner to grin at her.

She blinked at him.

"Did I forget to tell you?" he asked. "I'm coming with you."

She closed her eyes. "You just couldn't resist the opportunity to jump out and surprise me, could you? I think you have a problem with that."

He only grinned bigger. "Maybe. But aren't you glad to see me?"

It *was* awfully nice to see a familiar face.

"Only if it means I can kick your ass at boxing."

They hadn't yet faced off against each other with that sport, yet. It wasn't her best, but she was pretty sure she could take him.

"Boxing? I'm fantastic at boxing. You're on." He gestured for her to follow him. "I'll show you to your cabin. They're a little cramped, but they'll do. We'll stop at an outpost in about a week and hop on another ship."

As she followed him down the corridor, she rubbed the slender bracelet around her wrist—the one Peregrine had made for their team. When activated, it would alert her to the presence of her teammates thanks to the transmitters embedded in their tattoos.

She'd see them again soon.

She activated her bracelet.

MESSAGE FROM THE AUTHOR

Thank you for reading!

If you enjoyed this story and can spare a minute or two to leave a review on Amazon, I'd be grateful. It makes a big difference.

If you're ready for more Chains of Command, check out Cut to the Bone. Cut off from her team, Fallon's about to face her biggest challenge.

Be sure to visit www.ZenDiPietro.com and sign up for Zen's newsletter so you'll never miss a new release or sale. Stay tuned for more adventures!

I hope to hear from you!

In gratitude,
    Zen DiPietro

ABOUT THE AUTHOR

Zen DiPietro is a lifelong bookworm, dreamer, and writer. Perhaps most importantly, a Browncoat Trekkie Whovian. Also red-haired, left-handed, and a vegetarian geek. Absolutely terrible at conforming. A recovering gamer, but we won't talk about that. Particular loves include badass heroines, British accents, and the smell of Band-Aids.

www.ZenDiPietro.com.

DRAGONFIRE STATION UNIVERSE

Original Series (complete)
Dragonfire Station Book 1: Translucid
Dragonfire Station Book 2: Fragments
Dragonfire Station Book 3: Coalescence

Intersections (Dragonfire Station Short Stories)

Mercenary Warfare series (complete)
Selling Out
Blood Money
Hell to Pay
Calculated Risk
Going for Broke

Chains of Command series
New Blood
Blood and Bone
Cut to the Bone
Out for Blood

To get updates on releases and sales, sign up for Zen's newsletter.

Printed in Dunstable, United Kingdom